PREY'N JUSTICE

BY

ANGELA CHAPMAN

"PREY'N JUSTICE" by Angela Chapman ISBN 978-0-9845362-3-8

Published 2010 by Fire Pit Creek Publishing, 31208 E. Heidelberger Rd. Buckner M0. 64016 US. ©2010, Angela Chapman. All rights reserved. No part of this publication may be reproduced, stored in retrieval system, or transmitted in any form or by any means, electronic, mechanical, recording or otherwise, without the prior written permission of Angela Chapman.

Book cover designed by: Angela Chapman and Brady Jobe
Edited by: Candy Myers
Critiqued By: Brittney Jobe and Troy Sawyer

Manufactured in United States of America

This is for my mother, Lela Bryant--for always believing in me. And for Reverend Keith Hall--for guiding me in the right direction.

Chapter One

"You'll never be nothing! Do you hear me? You ain't ever going to amount to shit!" Sheila slurred.

"Well, at least I won't be drunk all the time and living in a hell hole like this," Jodie shouted. It was days like these that she wished she didn't even have a mom. She'd only been home from school five minutes, and all hell had broken loose.

Shaking her finger, Sheila stumbled awkwardly toward Jodie. "You listen to me, young lady. You just better be damn thankful you have somewhere to sleep. If you don't watch that smart tongue of yours, you're going to be out on the street like your sister."

"Nicole chose to leave—because of you!"

"Your sister's a slut, and you know it!

"No mom, you're the slut!" Jodie instantly regretted her words.

Sheila eyes narrowed as she lunged toward her. She grabbed a handful of Jodie's hair and pulled her head forward. "You unthankful bitch!"

Jodie cringed as she tugged on her mother's arms. "Ouch, let go of my hair!" She twisted and pulled until her hair came loose from her mother's grasp. She cradled her head and dropped to her knees.

Her mother staggered forward, knocking Jodie backwards and landing on top of her. She straddled Jodie, crushing her fists into her chest.

4

Jodie's face reddened and with all her strength, she shoved her mother off and jumped to her feet. "I hate you!" she screamed. She snatched her purse and jacket off the worn recliner. "Why do you have to be my mom?" She darted toward the front door.

Sheila grasped the arm of the couch and pulled herself onto her wobbly knees. "Get the hell out of my sight. Don't you dare come back here!"

Jodie whirled around and glared at her mom. "My friggen pleasure!" She slammed the door to the apartment and rushed down the hallway, past all the multi-colored graffiti scribbled across the walls. She usually liked to analyze the markings to make sure there weren't any new gang members lurking around the building, but this time she marched on by. Every few seconds, she glanced back over her shoulder. She was more worried that some pervert would reach out and pull her into his apartment than she was of her drunken mother stumbling after her. She knew there were at least two sexual offenders living in the building and probably more that she wasn't aware of. The aged building was full of thugs, junkies, and ex-convicts.

Maddie, a petite five-foot hundred pound elderly, black lady opened her door halfway and poked her head out. "Are you okay, Jodanne?" Her solemn black eyes lingered on Jodie before traveling the length of the hallway.

"I'm fine. Mom's just drunk again." Jodie hated it when Maddie called her by her real name. She only did that when she was concerned. Jodie's real name was Jodanne Josephine James. She imagined her mother was drunk or high when she named her the ludicrous name. If Jodie wasn't being teased for being poor, she was ridiculed because of her name. She wished she had a common name like her sister, Nicole Leah James.

"You poor thing. Come in and I'll fix you dinner." Maddie opened the door wider.

Although Maddie's funds were low because of the inadequate amount of her monthly social security check, she still continued to cram cookies and snacks into Jodie's hands whenever she passed by her apartment.

If someone had told Jodie five years ago that her best friend would end up being a sixty-year-old widow lady, she'd never have believed them. Although Maddie was distant in many ways—she was still the only person that Jodie would trust in a dark alley.

Maddie had recently lost her only son. He'd been mixed up with a gang and was killed in a drive by shooting right outside their apartment building.

"Thanks Maddie, but I'm not in the mood to eat." As sweet as the old lady was, Jodie knew she wasn't one you could walk all over. Rumor had it that after her son Jerome was killed, Maddie hunted down the gang member who had shot him and wasted him in the same fashion. Jodie didn't know how true it was, but she didn't put it past her. She'd witnessed once before Maddie chasing gang members out of the apartment building with a loaded rifle. She'd cursed up a storm as she threatened to blow their heads off. Jodie was shocked to hear gentle-spirited Maddie speaking in such a manner, but it had worked—the gang scattered. Of course, they came back the next day and started a fire in the hallway. Although there was no proof that it was that particular gang, Maddie and Jodie had no doubt that it was. Luckily, the fire was discovered before any major damage was done.

"You going out there?" Maddie's face remained somber as she nodded her head toward the lobby door.

"I've got to get away from this dump and *her*!" Jodie rolled her eyes toward the end of the hall.

Maddie glanced at her watch. "It'll be dark in a few hours. You know what the streets are like after dark, girl!"

"I'll be fine, Maddie." An unintentional tear escaped down Jodie's cheek. She flicked it away and patted her purse. "Don't worry, I got my mace."

Maddie rested her hands on her hips and shook her head as if she wasn't satisfied with Jodie's response. "Wait here." She disappeared into the apartment. A few minutes later, she returned. "Step inside." She pulled Jodie inside the apartment and glanced nervously up and down the hall before pulling the door closed. "I know I shouldn't be doing this, but it's a wicked world out there anymore, and your mace won't faze the determined criminal." She slid a small silver pistol into Jodie's hand. "Jerome gave me this before he died. It's a Barrette 25. He said I might need it to protect myself. I thought he was just being foolish." She glanced toward the ceiling. "God rest his soul—he must have known something was going to happen to him." Maddie's eyes hardened. "I want you to have it, and my God, use it if you have to."

"I can't take this! What if you need it?"

"Hush, child. I have my rifle; besides, I hardly get out anymore since Charlie started delivering my groceries."

"I don't know a thing about guns." Jodie's face paled as the earlier confrontation with her mom grew trivial. The gun could come in handy the next time her mom tried to beat her up—she'd love to threaten her mother in the same manner that she was used to. She glanced up at Maddie—she was stunned that the old lady was giving her a gun.

"I'll show you how to use it. But you got to promise me that your mother never finds out about it."

It was as if Maddie had read her mind. "I promise—she'll never know I have it."

"Watch, here's the clip." Maggie pulled the clip out of the pistol. "The bullets slide right in it, like so." She continued to show Jodie how to load the pistol. "I have extra bullets, but hopefully, you'll never need them."

"I don't know what to say…"

"You don't have to say anything. Just take care of yourself and do what you have to do." Maddie took a step backwards. "Now let me see…" She studied Jodie from head to toe. "You don't want to carry it in your purse—in case you're mugged. How about your jacket? Do you have a pocket without holes?"

"I do. I have a pocket on the inside of my coat."

"Perfect. Carry it there." She poked her finger at Jodie's chest. "Now remember, I'm trusting you, girl. Don't do anything foolish with it."

"You can trust me, Maddie."

7

Maddie's voice softened, "You know if you ever need somewhere to sleep, you can stay here—until your mother sobers up, that is. Otherwise, she'd have the cops at my door. You understand what I'm saying, don't you?"

"I do, and thanks, but I'll be fine." Jodie tucked the gun into her jacket. "I gotta go."

"Be careful, Jodie. I don't need…" Maddie's voice faltered as her eyes locked with Jodie's. "Just be careful."

Jodie sensed Maddie wanted to say more, but for some reason had changed her mind. She said good-bye and promised Maddie that she would stop by tomorrow.

Jodie stepped outside the building just as a gust of wind hit her in the face. She was glad she'd grabbed her jacket for *two* reasons now. Usually New York was warmer in April, but it had been chilly every day, and the month was nearly over.

She tucked her hands in her pockets as she paused on the top stair. A few steps down sat Gino and Winky, a couple of harmless cokeheads. Jodie always wondered how they managed to stay out of gang activity. She knew that it wasn't an easy task around this part of the city. Although they weren't a threat, Jodie wasn't in any mood to have a conversation with them.

The stairs were wide, so she stepped down on the opposite side. She was hoping they were too stoned to notice her. However, her plan failed.

Gino glanced over his shoulder and quickly stood. His long dark hair tumbled over his shoulders, and his outgrown bangs fell over his eyes. "Why check her out, Wink…" He whistled. "Damn Jodie—how about you and I going out tonight?"

Jodie rolled her eyes. "I don't think so."

Winky snickered. "Oh man, she doesn't want to go out with your sorry ass." He flexed the muscles in his chest and winked at Jodie. "It's a real man you need, honey. Take me for example." He leaned forward and rested his elbow on his knee. "One night with me, and you'll be begging for more."

"You keep talking trash, and I won't be able to eat my supper." Jodie couldn't imagine any woman sleeping with Winky even if she was being paid high dollars to do so. His

8

breath alone would kill you—it reeked of whiskey and cigars. Although he had a halfway descent physique, his face was pitted and the majority of his teeth were missing. Unlike Gino, he wore his long bleached blond hair pulled back in a ponytail. His sleeves were rolled up and on his left arm was an eye winking with the name 'Winky' tattooed underneath it.

Jodie could tell they both were stoned out of their heads. She didn't recall ever seeing them sober.

Gino giggled childishly. "Shut up Wink…you know I'm the mack daddy on the block."

Jodie shook her head. "Later, guys." She hurried up the street, ignoring Winky's pleas to stick around.

The sun was still shining, and the block was still active, but that would all change in a few hours. Jodie glanced across the street at three young girls, chanting while jumping rope, their pigtails bouncing in rhythm with each jump. Her eyes lingered on the girls as she thought of her own childhood. She couldn't remember ever having friends to play with. The only fond memories she had were of her and Nicole hanging out after school while her mother bar hopped. It was during those times that she and Nicole watched TV together or did their homework. Sometimes they would act silly and pretend to be the actors on the sitcoms, and other times they were more serious and talked about their dreams. Jodie's smile faded as she recalled her mother coming home from the bars. Although Jodie and Nicole would clean the house every day, it was never done well enough for their drunken mother. Her mother always took her anger out on Nicole since she was the oldest.

Jodie blinked back tears. She missed Nicole—she'd quit school last year as soon as she turned sixteen, and left home. Jodie knew that she was working in Astoria, Queens, selling her body to survive. Rumor had it that she was working for J.J. Saughter, one of the harshest pimps in New York City. It saddened Jodie; she knew it wasn't the life that Nicole had intended—she'd always dreamed of being a nurse. Now her dreams would never come true.

9

Jodie's sixteenth birthday was in six months, and she was determined not to follow in Nicole's footsteps, no matter how horrid her life became with her mother. Her mother's words echoed in her head, 'you ain't ever going to amount to shit.' *You wait and see if I don't,* Jodie told herself. She lifted her chin and crossed the street. She turned the corner and scurried up the alley. She knew exactly where she was going: the only spot left that the gangs hadn't found and claimed as their territory and the only place in the world where she could be alone with her thoughts.

The alley was empty with the exception of a sleek black cat leaping on top of a garbage can. Jodie pinched her nose; the smell of garbage reeked. The alley was cluttered with weathered car parts, and rusted cans were scattered around the trash bin. The alley hadn't been cleaned for years, not since she'd been in the neighborhood anyway.

An elderly, bearded man stumbled out of the back door of an apartment building, clutching a bottle in a paper sack. "Hey, honey, where've you been? Are you the mail lady?" He burped loudly and covered his mouth. "You got my check?"

Jodie increased her speed and crossed over to the opposite side. She didn't bother to glance back at the old geezer; she knew he was in no condition to catch up with her.

She came to the end of the alley and rounded the corner, keeping her eyes alert. She glanced up at the deteriorating apartment building and wondered how much longer before the building was declared hazardous. Most the landlords in the area continue to rent out the poorly maintained apartments as long as they could get by with it.

She edged her way around the backside of the building and quickly slid behind the bush that camouflaged the basement window. Jodie pulled the boards off that were secured loosely over the window and lowered herself through it. She quickly placed the boards back from the inside.

She slid her hand over the top of a cardboard box until she felt the candle. She pulled a lighter out of her purse and lit it.

She'd discovered the hideaway last year when she had, somehow, navigated into the vicinity of a gang fight. As soon as she'd realized what was taking place, she'd slithered quietly behind the bush, so she wouldn't be seen and that's when she discovered the broken window. She'd easily pulled the boards off and slid inside until the gang banging was over.

The room had been empty with the exception of a few boxes of rusted cooking pans. There had been no signs of graffiti, so she was certain no one else had discovered the place. From that day on, she claimed the secret place as her own.

Jodie sat down in the center of the cot and pulled the blanket over her legs. She lit a cigarette, took a long drag, and blew the smoke out slowly. If only every moment in life could be as pleasurable as the first hit off a cigarette. She leaned back against the wall and glanced around the candle-lit room. It had taken a while, but her little niche finally felt cozy, although it wasn't any bigger than a restroom. She had gotten brave one afternoon and stole the cot off a back porch, and she'd used the cardboard boxes to make a coffee table.

Many nights she'd slept on the cot because of her mother's drunken rage or one-night stands. Jodie didn't particularly like staying there after dark, not only because it was cold but also scary. But some nights she just didn't have a choice. She patted the pocket where the pistol was. Now she would be a little less frightened. She knew there was always the chance of someone finding her hideout. The nights that she'd slept over she'd lined the rusted pans along the window's ledge. In the event there was an intruder, the crashing pots and pans would wake her. She always kept her mace within reach, too.

Jodie had tried to open the only door in the room, but stacked boxes on the opposite side were shoved up against it. She imagined the basement was once used for storage but had been abandoned over the years. The boxes made her feel more secure because she knew the door would be invisible from the other side, but if she needed to escape fast, she was sure she could muscle the boxes enough to squeeze through it. But for now, she didn't see any reason to force the door open.

11

She stubbed the cigarette out in an ashtray and picked up the magazine off the homemade coffee table. She flipped through the pages of teenaged celebrities as hunger pains set in. She thought of the peanut butter and bread in the cabinet at home and wished she'd had time to eat a sandwich. She imagined if she waited a few hours her mom would pass out, and she could sneak back into the apartment. Her mother would never remember the recent incident in the morning.

She stared for a long moment at the picture of Mischa Barton in a designer outfit, which consisted of a blue mini skirt with a matching halter-top and a silver-studded jacket.

She tossed the magazine on the box and stretched out across the cot. She closed her eyes as she imagined herself in fashionable clothes and waving to fans as she crawled out of a limo. A young good-looking man came up to stand by her. He brushed her lips with his before escorting her into the extravagant club.

Just the thought of being in love aroused Jodie. Her eyes fluttered opened and her lips curved into a smile. She pulled the cover up over her shoulders.

One day her life would be different. She'd have nice things and eat at fancy restaurants—as long as she could keep her life on the right track. So far, she'd managed to keep out of gangs and keep her grades good, although it'd been a challenge.

She imagined the perfect future with a mate that loved her unconditionally. Her eyes slowly closed as her mind drifted back to the gorgeous man whirling her around on the dance floor, and before long, she was fast asleep and relishing the dream.

Chapter Two

Tara twirled a strand of hair around her finger as she gazed out the window at the street below. Some boys were playing dodge ball against the building, while the girls at the end of the block were jumping rope. Two longhair greasers were sitting on the steps across the street. A lady came out and called up the street toward the young girls. A taxi pulled up and an elderly man crawled out with a bag of groceries. After a while, the dim streetlights flickered on, and all the youngsters disappeared into the apartments. The activities slowly ceased.

She couldn't believe a week ago she was sitting in her trendy lavender bedroom in Troy, New York, emailing her friends on the Internet, and now she was sitting in a run-down dump in the lower East side of New York City all alone. "It isn't fair," she mumbled as tears surfaced. She'd cried so much in the last week she'd thought she was all dried up.

She still blamed herself for her parents' fatal accident. If only she hadn't called them to meet her at the mall. Her parents had agreed to buy her a new stereo for her fifteenth birthday, so she'd gone with her friend Lacy to the mall and found an incredible deal on a hi-fi stereo.

Tara rubbed her temples as the horrible images materialized. All she'd wanted was to get her parents approval. It was a perfectly gorgeous Saturday; the streets were dryer than ever. *Then why couldn't the truck stop from sliding into mom and dad's SUV?* She'd asked herself that question a thousand times.

The truck driver lost control of his vehicle, crossed the media, and slid into her parent's Trailblazer. The blazer skidded off the embankment and rolled several times down the hill. Her parents were pronounced dead at the scene.

Tara pulled a tissue out of her pocket and blew her nose.

The only relative she had in New York was her dad's brother, Tommy. She had a few aunts, uncles, and cousins in Denver, where her mother grew up, but Tara had never met them.

Uncle Tommy didn't hesitate to take Tara in, although he didn't have much to offer. Being a single thirty-year-old man with a limited income, he'd settled on a one-bedroom apartment in a run-down part of the city. The inhabitants were poor and ethnically mixed. Until the will was settled and a claim for the insurance filed, Tara would have to reside in Tommy's shabby apartment.

She'd arrived a day earlier with just a few bags of her personal belongings. The rest had gone into storage. Unfortunately, her parents didn't have credit life on their house. She vaguely remembered a conversation one night at dinner, her mother had told her father the insurance had expired and he needed to switch the house over, but Tara's dad, known for procrastinating, never got it done.

Tara crossed over to the kitchen cupboard. She pulled the doors opened and stared at the contents: one can of ravioli, one can of spaghetti, two cans of corn, a bag of potato chips, and a loaf of bread. She didn't bother to open the refrigerator because she already knew what was in there—leftover KFC chicken, which she'd eaten earlier for lunch, a package of salami, hotdogs, and a carton of milk. Tommy told her he'd be stopping by the store when he got off work.

She glanced at the oval clock on the TV—it was after nine. Her uncle's shift at the convenience store was from 1:00 p.m. to 9:30 p.m. She figured by the time he got groceries it would be after ten before he got home. She hadn't eaten dinner and her stomach rumbled loudly.

14

Tommy had left a ten-dollar bill and told her not to go further than the corner market a couple blocks away, and not to go out after dark.

With it being Friday, she had the whole weekend to settle in before enrolling in school on Monday. She was already thinking about writing her friends from Troy. Her uncle couldn't afford the Internet, so she couldn't email her friends on her laptop, and her cell phone had been shut off until the bill was paid so calling was out. She wasn't about to make long distant calls on Tommy's phone and run his bill up. She would have to settle for writing letters the old fashion way—that is if she'd thought to pack her notebook paper.

She strolled back to the window. The narrow streets were empty except for two young Hispanic teenaged boys walking up the center of the street. They were dressed in jeans and t-shirts. Other than the two boys, the street was deserted. The boys looked harmless and soon they were out of sight.

Tara cracked the window to let the cool breeze in. Although she couldn't see the main strip, she could hear the cars in the distance.

She glanced again at the clock as she cogitated whether to go against her uncle's wishes and run down to the corner market to get a notebook and something appealing to eat. She still had time to get back before he got home, and he would just assume she went to the store earlier in the day. The thought of sitting in the apartment on a Friday night watching basic channels on TV helped to finalize her decision. She'd have to hurry though. She grabbed the money off the table and slid it into her jeans pocket. She grabbed her lightweight windbreaker, threw it on, and hurried out the door. As soon as she stepped outside, she wished she'd worn a heavier jacket—it was chillier and *darker* than she'd thought.

Tara pulled the jacket tighter around her and headed in the direction of the store. The night was eerie, the quarter moon was barely visible, and the silence was so thick she could hear a horsefly buzzing nearby.

15

A hundred feet later, she froze; the blaring music from a stereo convinced her she was no longer alone. She spun around and spotted a car's headlights at the end of the block. She couldn't make out how many guys were hanging around the car. She prayed it wasn't a gang. She'd never had an encounter with a gang member and hoped she didn't have one tonight. She didn't think to ask Tommy if there were gangs in the vicinity. "Duh," she mumbled under her breath. Maybe that was why Tommy didn't want her to go out after dark. She quickened her pace and suddenly wished she'd taken her uncle's advice. She glanced back over her shoulder; the apartment wasn't even a block away. She could always turn back, but then she would be going in the direction of the car. Right now, she was out of view of the streetlight, but she wouldn't be if she went back. She slowed her pace as she struggled what to do.

A snapping sound on the side of the apartment building startled her. It sounded like someone stepped on a branch. Someone could have come from the alley and be lurking near the side of the building. She shivered as she shifted her gaze toward the darkness; she strained to see if she could make out any kind of shadow, but it was too dark. *That's it; I'm going back,* she thought. If she ran fast, maybe the guys at the end of the block wouldn't bother her. She had to try anyway.

She spun around, but her breath caught in her throat as a dark figure lunged toward her. She managed a muffled scream just as a club caught the side of her head. She swung wildly into the air as she fell to her knees. Her vision blurred as the blood trickled down the side of her face. *Where was he?*

Suddenly, he was behind her, pinning her arms together and dragging her around the side of the building. She tried to scream but only desperate sobs escaped. *Where was he taking her?* She fought and kicked, but he was too strong. She moaned as her jacket and shirt hiked up, and sharp gravel dug into her back. *The alley?* She fought to stay conscious, but her head was swarming.

Tara was vaguely aware of a strong foul odor. She blinked as he pulled her beside a trash bin and bonded her hands together with duct tape. Her eyes grew heavy again. She couldn't keep

16

them open—she was exhausted. The excruciating pain was weakening her. She was sure she'd die if she didn't stay awake.

She forced her eyes open. After a few seconds, her blurred vision diminished, and she could make out his face. He was young, maybe twenty—his skin was smooth and dark, and his eyes black as the night. Although he wore a red stocking cap, the head of a snake tattoo was visible on the lower part of his forehead. The snake had diamond shapes and was copper color; its tongue was twisted and ready to strike. Tara wondered if the tattoo was a symbol of the thug's lifestyle. She moaned and tried to scoot away, but her back stung, and her head was throbbing. She felt like she'd been run over by a car. But she was sure being hit by a car would be far better than being captive of this monster. She stared desperately into his cold eyes and forced her lips apart. "Please, please," she begged, "don't hurt me."

He didn't respond. Tara winced as he ripped the front of her shirt. *Oh God, help me,* she prayed. *He's going to rape me!* She screamed with all the strength she could muster up, but a sudden switchblade at her throat silenced her.

He ran the tip of the knife down her throat onto her chest until it reached the center of her bra.

Tara bit down so hard on her bottom lip that she could taste the bitterness from the blood. She could feel her body trembling on the cold, rough ground.

He quickly slit the bra in the center so her breasts were exposed.

She laid in terror. She was too scared to move. He still didn't speak, but Tara knew from his fierce manner that he probably wouldn't hesitate to kill her. And as the tears slid off the side of her cheeks onto the ground, she wondered if he would kill her anyway when he was finished with her.

She cringed and bit down harder on her lip as he fumbled with the button on her jeans. She knew what was next. She couldn't believe this was happening after the horrible ordeal she'd just went through last week. *Why didn't she listen to Tommy?* The queasiness in her stomach increased. She could feel his body harden as he anxiously tugged on her jeans. She twisted again, trying to pull away, but once again, the knife was brought to her throat.

She stiffened and held her breath. He gradually removed the knife and laid it down on the ground as he finished pulling her jeans down. She squeezed her eyes shut. *Oh God, please save me,* she prayed.

His hand groped her breast.

She forced her eyes opened and gasped. Her startled gaze traveled passed his ruthless face toward a tall, lean dark-hair Hispanic girl, standing twenty feet behind them. For a second, she thought she was hallucinating.

The girl jerked a small pistol from her jacket and pointed it toward the back of the black guy. "Get the hell off her. So help me, I'll blow you're friggen head off."

The guy jumped to his feet, grabbed the knife on the ground, and spun around to face his assailant. He held the switchblade out in front of him as if he was an animal defending his prey. "You better split, bitch."

"No, you better get out of here, or they're going to be carrying your ass out of here in a body bag." The girl's eyes narrowed as she stood her ground.

"Do you even know how to use that thing?" The guy didn't budge.

Tara glanced toward the sky. *Please, please, please, God, help this girl save me.*

"If you're not out of here in five seconds you're going to find out!" The girl positioned her legs apart and squinted one eye shut as if she was ready to fire.

The guy hesitated.

"One, two, three…" she counted.

"Bitch! You haven't heard the end of me!" He grunted, flipped the switchblade closed, and disappeared around the side of the building.

The girl waited until he was out of sight and quickly tucked the pistol back in her jacket. She hurried toward Tara and ripped the tape from around her hands.

"Thank you, thank you," Tara sobbed. She stood, pulled her jeans up, and then fastened the jacked over her bare chest. "I was so scared. I thought he was going to kill me."

"He probably would have. It's not unusual for a cop to find a dead body in this alley." She tipped Tara's chin to look at her head. "That's a nasty gash." She glanced up and down the alley. "We need to get out of here before he comes back with his own gun—or worse, more of his buddies."

"I live with my uncle." Tara's snivels ceased. "Will you please take me home?"

"Let's go. We've got to hurry."

Tara stayed close behind the girl as they rounded the building. She occasionally clutched on to the girl's shirt as she glanced nervously back over her shoulder. Although she was reasonably relieved, she was still paranoid that the maniac was hiding nearby and waiting to jump her again.

The girl hesitated and scooted closer to the building out of view of the streetlights. Tara did the same and pointed toward the tall building her uncle lived in. She was glad to see the carload of guys from earlier were gone. She wondered if her assailant had been with them.

The girl whispered. "Have your key ready. It looks safe, but let's run anyway. You ready?"

Tara trembled as she fumbled to find the key in her jean pocket. She was thankful it was still there. She nodded. All she wanted was to get inside of Tommy's as fast as possible.

"Okay, let's go," the girl said.

They ran toward the building, up the stairs, and inside. The girl motioned Tara to take the lead.

Tara couldn't stop the tears as she shoved the key into the lock. She couldn't quit thinking about what the girl had said about the thug killing her. She pushed the door open and they both stumbled inside, slamming the door behind them. She quickly locked the door.

Tara sobbed as she glanced at the ceiling. "Oh God, thank you." She hugged the girl. "God heard my prayers and sent you to rescue me. Thank you so much."

19

"I don't think that's what happened." She rolled her eyes and walked over to the window to glance out. "I was trying to sneak home quietly, and I thought I heard sobbing. As soon as I saw the back of the dude, I knew what was up."

Tara immediately noticed the embedded dimple in the girl's left cheek. "I am so grateful! My name is Tara."

"You can call me Jodie." She wiped the sweat from her hands onto her jeans. "You've got anything I can clean your wound with?

Tara wiped at the blood that was still oozing down the side of her face. "I was so scared—I forgot all about my head." She led Jodie into the bathroom and rummaged through the cabinet until she found some Peroxide, Neosporin, and bandages. She sat on the toilet lid as Jodie doctored her wound. "My uncle will be here soon. He's going to be pissed when he finds out what happened. He told me not to go out after dark."

"You're uncle knows what he's talking about. It's like committing suicide to venture around this neighborhood after dark without a weapon."

"Why were you out?" Tara asked puzzled.

Jodie hesitated, and Tara wondered if she was going to share the information.

Jodie finally spoke. "I figured I was safer on the streets than at home."

"I'm sorry. It's none of my business. I'm just so glad you were around to save me." Tara stood and lifted her jacket. "How's my back look?"

"You've got some cuts." Jodie yanked a small pebble out of Tara's back and continued to doctor it. She finished and handed Tara the Neosporin. "Well, I need to get home now before it gets any later."

"You're not serious, are you? You can't go back out there."

Jodie scurried to the window again. "It's pretty quiet right now, which is odd for a Friday night." She hesitated and seemed to be lost in thought. "Almost spooky." She glanced toward Tara. "Anyway, I'm sure it will liven up before the night is over. It's best if I go now. I live directly across from you." She pointed

20

toward the towering, dingy building on the opposite side of the street.

"Oh, I'm glad you live close. Well, if you're sure you don't want to wait for my uncle."

"I'm sure. You're safe now—just don't go out after dark anymore. And maybe you shouldn't be out walking by yourself either." She rested her hands on her hips. "A matter of fact, I guess I probably shouldn't either as long as that hoodlum is prowling around. We need to take his threat serious."

"Do you want to catch the bus with me in the mornings for school?" Tara asked. "I just arrived yesterday. My uncle was planning to enroll me on Monday. You can ride with us if you want."

"That might be wise. The loser will forget about us in a couple of weeks and move on to something else destructive."

"I'm sure my uncle will call the police and report the incident when he comes home." Tara followed Jodie to the door.

"I don't know if I'd recommend that. If the guy gets in trouble with the law, he might get all his scumbag friends after you. If you plan to live in this neighborhood, you just better be thankful nothing more happened, and drop it."

Tara was stunned by Jodie's words. She was almost raped and would have probably been killed. She wondered if Jodie would *really* dismiss the situation if it had been her. "I don't know if my uncle will settle for doing nothing."

"If he's been around the vicinity for awhile, I'm sure he will. I don't mean to sound callous, but it's just a fact—life is hell around here." Jodie unlocked the door and stepped into the hallway cautiously. "I'll talk to you sometime this weekend about Monday. Be sure to lock up."

"Okay. I'll watch you from the window. Thanks for everything." Tara closed the door, locked it, and hurried over to the window. She watched Jodie run across the street, up the stairs, and disappear into the building.

She crossed over to the bathroom and studied the reflection in the mirror. Her short sandy-blond hair was matted from the blood. Her once lively blue eyes were swollen, and mascara was

21

smudged across her cheeks. She could see the early stages of bruising around the bandage. She touched her lip and flinched; dried blood had settled in the cracks. She was sure by morning the swelling would be worse, and she'd resemble a face of a body being pulled from a river. The tears came slowly and then more rapidly as she stared at the horrid image. Her words came in spurts in between the sobs, "Why momma? Why daddy? Why did you leave me? Why is this happening to me? I want to go home!"

Chapter Three

Jodie flipped over and glanced at the alarm clock. It was almost noon. She hadn't meant to sleep so late. She kicked the covers off, threw her legs over the edge of the bed, and sat up. She yawned and stretched her arms above her head. Her mind wandered to the girl across the street. Although it wasn't her usual nature to feel sympathy for people, she couldn't help but feel sorry for Tara. How awful to be new to the neighborhood and have an experience like she'd had so suddenly. Jodie knew Tara wasn't street smart and would struggle to survive in this part of the city.

She stood, grabbed her jeans off the chair, and pulled them on. She had a sudden urge to check on her, but she silently warned herself not to get too involved. She wasn't cut out to be anybody's bodyguard. Tara would have to toughen up on her own just like she had to do.

Jodie finished dressing, brushed her teeth, and ran the brush through her lengthy tangled hair. She quietly slipped down the hallway and peeked in her mother's room. Her mom was sprawled out across the bed snoring loudly. Sometimes after a night of heavy drinking, her mother wouldn't wake up until late into the afternoon.

Jodie hurried back to the kitchen and rummaged through her mother's purse. She spotted a twenty and tucked it into her jeans. She threw her jacket on, although she didn't think she'd need it. She needed somewhere to hide her new toy. She crossed back to her bedroom and grabbed the gun from under her mattress. She slipped out the door and across the street to Tara's building.

Jodie raised her hand to knock on the door, but her doubled up fist froze in midair as a series of doubts surfaced. Maybe Tara wouldn't be in the mood for company after her terrorizing ordeal, or maybe she was still sleeping. Jodie wished she'd thought this through first. After a few more seconds, she shrugged and knocked on the door. She'd always been one to act on impulse—*why change now.*

After a few seconds, she heard distant footsteps patter toward the door and then sudden silence. Jodie waited silently. Baffled, she knocked again.

Finally, after several seconds she heard Tara's soft voice. "Yeah?"

"Tara, it's me, Jodie."

Tara cracked the door and peered through. She grinned and opened the door wider. "Hi, Jodie. Sorry for the delay. I freaked for a second—I thought you might be that hoodlum coming back to finish me off."

"I don't think he'd have the balls to come to your door." Jodie stepped into the living room. She glanced casually around the cluttered room to avoid looking at Tara's swollen face. "I just wanted to come by and check on you. Is your uncle here? Everything cool with him?"

"He's gone right now. He had some errands to run before he went to work." Tara motioned Jodie to sit on the couch. "He was pretty upset. He promised as soon as the insurance money comes we'd moved to a better neighborhood."

"Insurance money?"

"Yeah. I didn't get a chance to tell you last night, my parents were killed in an auto accident last week and..." Tara words drifted off and she turned away.

"Oh wow! I didn't know. I'm sorry."

"That's okay," she said in a raspy voice. "I'm pushing though it slowly."

"Well, how about I take you somewhere for lunch down on the strip?" *Where the hell did that come from,* Jodie wondered.

24

She'd had no intention of coming over here and asking Tara for lunch. She'd had other plans for her twenty—like smokes and playing pool tonight at Chester's Pool House. She didn't know what possessed her to ask Tara for lunch. Yeah, she did—her freaking impulsive behavior again, a frustrating habit that she couldn't seem to kick.

"That's really nice of you. I haven't eaten yet."

"Grab your stuff and let's rock and roll." Jodie glanced at her watch. If they hurry, they could still catch the lunch special at Tulipano's Café. It's good, inexpensive Italian food. She sighed silently. She decided not to fret over the money because she knew she could always hustle pool, or steal some liquor and resell it to the minors loitering the block. "You like Italian?"

"I love it! Let me leave my uncle a note." Tara grabbed the pen off the counter and scribbled onto the notepad. "He made me promise not to leave the house alone. He won't mind if I'm with you. I told him all about you and what you did last night. He said he's going to come by and thank you when he gets a chance."

"That's not necessary."

"I know, but he's a man of his word." Tara suddenly gasped, "I can't go with you!" She spun around to face Jodie. "Did you happen to notice? I look like a beast! I can't go out in public looking like this."

"Sure you can. Where's your makeup?"

"I don't think it will help." Tara led Jodie to the bathroom and pointed to the satchel.

Jodie grabbed the bag and motioned Tara to sit at the kitchen table. She carefully covered Tara's black and blue marks with foundation, and then applied blue eye shadow, so the bruises weren't nearly as visible. She outlined the bottom of her eyes in black and dotted her cheeks lightly with blush. She took a step back to inspect her creation. "You can barely tell the difference. Check it out."

Tara examined her face in the mirror. "Wow, I do look better. Well, then I don't have any other excuse." She scooped her keys off the table. "I'm ready." Her face suddenly paled. "You don't think that thug will be lurking around, do you?"

"More than likely he partied all night and is still sleeping. But if not, I still have my friend with me." Jodie grinned and patted her jacket pocket, but Tara's gloom expression didn't alter. "C'mon, you can't live in fear the rest of your life. Let's go have some fun."

Tara smiled weakly. "You're right. Let's go."

Jodie wasn't fooled for a second. She knew Tara's smile was forced and that she was actually scared shitless. She had a sinking sensation that she was making a huge mistake—what if Tara decided to trail on her heels for now on out—like a scared puppy dog.

***

Jodie sighed and leaned back in the booth. The spaghetti had been delicious but filling. She lit a cigarette and held out the pack toward Tara.

"No thanks," Tara mumbled.

"Suit yourself. You don't know what you're missing. There's nothing like a cigarette after a good meal."

"My father would turn over in his grave."

"Yeah, well, you still don't know what you're missing." Jodie waived the waitress down to pay the ticket.

"What are we going to do now?" Tara asked eagerly. "I don't have much money, but I do still have the ten my uncle gave me last night."

Jodie was on the verge of asking her to pay for her own meal. But instead, she picked up her glass of tea and downed it. Tara didn't seem like the type that was used to being ridiculed—she'd probably crumble. "I don't care what we do. You got a fake ID?"

Tara's jaw dropped. "Of course not. I've never needed one."

"Well, there's not much to do without an ID. If Jack is in a good mood, he might let you in the pool hall as long as you don't drink." Jodie nodded to the waitress as she returned with the change. She dropped a dollar and the change on the table, and tucked the rest of the bills in her pocket

"I don't drink alcohol," Tara stated.

26

Jodie rolled her eyes. "You don't drink or smoke?" She stubbed her cigarette out in the ashtray. "Well, I don't drink that much myself. My mother seems to drink enough for the both of us!" She stood and Tara followed her outside. "Anyway, we can go over to Kingdom Hill and see what's happening over there."

"Kingdom Hill?"

"That's what we call it. It's a huge park with a basketball court. There's a place for kids to skateboard, too. A lot of teenagers hang out there. A few of them are decent, but I don't associate with any of them. I don't trust anyone any more!" Jodie made a 'cutting throat' gesture. "Remember, don't trust everyone you meet."

Tara's eyes widened. "Is it safe?"

"As long as you don't turn your back on anyone." The look on Tara's face was hilarious, and Jodie laughed. "I'm just kidding. Loosen up—it's daylight; we'll be fine."

Tara moaned in relief. "Okay, if you want to."

Jodie didn't try to carry on a conversation with Tara during their ten-minute walk. She wasn't accustomed to chatting with friends and found it a difficult task. She'd always wondered what friends could possibly talk about for long periods at a time. She'd already given Tara her life scoop while they ate their lunch.

"Do you have a boyfriend?" Tara asked.

"Nope."

"Have you ever had one?"

"Not really," Jodie said bluntly. She wasn't about to share her sex life with this girl.

"Do you have a crush on any guy at school?"

"None that I know of." Jodie felt like she was on trial and being interrogated for some crime.

"I liked this guy named Mick Kester in my old school. We decided to break up when he found out I was moving." She shrugged. "I guess it's for the best."

Jodie was glad to reach the slope leading to Kingdom Hill. As they strolled down the hill, she pointed to the right where the kids were skateboarding. She then nodded toward the basketball

27

game going on at the bottom of the hill, and the dozen spectators sitting on the poorly maintained bleachers. She crossed over to the other side of the street and led Tara to the park. "I usually like to walk through the park when I come. Sometimes I bring bread crumbs and feed the pigeons from the bench over there." She pointed to a green, faded wooden bench. "C'mon, let's go sit."

Tara glanced around wide-eyed. "This is how you spend your Saturdays?"

Jodie plopped down on the bench. "Not always, but it does gives me a break from the pool hall." She nodded toward a little blond hair girl with dirt smeared around her mouth, tugging at her mother's shirt, as the mother tried to coo another baby in the stroller. "I like to watch the kids playing and the mothers pushing their strollers through the park." Jodie's eyes shifted back to the basketball game. "Do you see those two Hispanic guys and the two gals with them on the bleachers?"

Tara nodded.

"I think they are part of a gang and up to no good. They've already approached me, but I wasn't into them at all. I'm sure they hang out here, trying to promote new members. I don't know where their turf is."

Tara's eyes remained on the four on the bleachers. "Wow, that's creepy! Are there a lot of gangs around here?"

"Are you kidding? Let's see—the Bloods, the Crips, Goodyear Crew, and the Netas, just to name a few. There's so much thug life going on anymore, and if you're not careful, you could get mixed up right along with them."

"Jodie, you're really scaring me."

"I'm sorry, but it's the truth." She lit a cigarette. "Don't worry, I'll teach you the language of thug-life and how to read the signs of the hood. That's why I brought you here. I think this is the only place that hasn't been taken over by the 'hood."

Tara's face suddenly paled, and she dug her fingernails into the side of Jodie's leg. "Omigod, look."

Jodie followed Tara's terrified gaze up the hill to the three black guys dressed in black nylon shorts and red jerseys. The

28

stout one on the end was carrying a basketball. Jodie's eyes settled on the middle one with the crew cut and a viscous-looking snake tattoo slithering out from under his headband. His dark vile eyes met hers, and for a brief second, Jodie wondered if he recognized her. She quickly turned her head, but not before she saw him nudge his buddy and nod in her direction. *He remembered.* She tried to swallow, but the saliva in her mouth suddenly grew dry. Goose bumps surfaced on the base of her neck as a sharp pain pierced her stomach. She felt for the budge on the inside of her jacket—the pistol was still there.

"Oh God, he going's to kill us!" Tara groaned.

Jodie's adrenaline rocketed, as she pulled Tara to her feet. "Just stay calm."

Tara's shallow breaths soon escalated into muffled sobs.

"Tara, please get a grip and don't look their way." She grasped Tara's hand and squeezed it. "Now, stay close to me and do as I do. He knows I'm strapped, so he'd be a fool to try anything out here."

"Where do we go?" Tara whispered.

"The opposite way they are. C'mon I know a short cut out of here." She led Tara to a less active side street, but suddenly changed her mind. She didn't think it would be wise to take off down a street where there weren't many people around. That's just what the thugs would want. They needed to stay in view of the crowds. "I changed my mind. We're going to go back up the hill but on the opposite side." She knew if they stayed on the main drag people would be close by at all times.

"No, Jodie. I don't want to."

"C'mon, it's our only choice unless you want to stick around in the park." She crossed over to the opposite side of the street, and Tara followed reluctantly. "What ever you do—don't look their way."

"Oh, I wish I would have stayed home." A single tear escaped down the side of Tara's cheek.

They made it half way up the hill before Jodie spotted them out of the corner of her eye, crossing over to their side of the street. She kept her hand on the inside of her jacket, prepared to

29

use the weapon if she needed to. She vowed to herself not to show any sign of weakness. She'd learned years ago if others know you are frightened, they'll feed upon you even more. You have to be tough to live in this part of the city, no matter how scared you are.

Jodie could tell by the snickering behind them that they were getting closer.

One of them commented, "Hey, homies, check out the bumper kits?"

Jodie heard them all chuckle. She'd been hanging on the streets long enough to know they were referring to their butts.

The guys edged closer. "Hey, bitch, let's see your bad ass now, or did you forget your gat?"

She easily recognized the deep voice from last night. She glanced at Tara—her nose was scrunched and her eyes were clouded with tears.

Jodie suddenly spun around, whipped the pistol out, and jerked it in his direction. Tara gasped along with a few other mothers in the park that were witnessing the incident. "You better leave us the hell alone," she yelled.

The guy held out his hands in front of the other two guys to stop them from advancing any further. "Bitch, you're fucked!"

Jodie remained silent as she kept the gun pointed toward him. Police sirens could be heard from a distance. She wasn't sure if someone had called the police, or if they were just in the vicinity, because of another crime. But whatever the reason, it was enough to rattle the thugs.

"C'mon, Snake, let's break before it's too late. We don't need any shit going down," the dude carrying the basketball shouted as he backed away.

Jodie now knew his nickname—Snake. She kept her stance and stared directly into his ruthless eyes. She held her breath and tightened her grip to lessen the vibration of the gun. She hoped he couldn't tell how much she was shaking. He stood there for what seemed like eternity. It was as if he was weighing all his options.

30

After a few more seconds, he doubled up his fist and shook it at Jodie. "Bitch, your going to wish you had never fucked with me." He spun on his heels and jogged after his friends.

Jodie sighed as she dropped her arms to her side.

Tara let out a fearful whimper and threw her arms around Jodie. "I was so scared."

The sirens were drawing nearer.

"C'mon, we don't have time to fart around." Jodie tucked the pistol back in her jacket and turned away from the accumulating crowd. "Let's run before I get busted." She broke into a hard run, and Tara followed.

After a few blocks, Jodie glanced over her shoulder and slowed down her pace. She noticed that Tara was heaving and tears were streaming down her cheeks.

"I can't run any more." Tara doubled over and rested her hands on her knees as she gasped for air.

"It's okay; I think we're in the clear now. Just rest a minute."

"What are we going to do?" Tara glanced up, wide-eyed. "He's never going to leave us alone. He's always going to be after us."

"C'mon, we can walk now. Don't worry—I'll think of something." Jodie took one last glance over her shoulder as chills traveled down her spine. She couldn't shake the image of his piercing dark eyes and his crooked grin as he warned her that he wasn't finished with her. She didn't have the heart to tell Tara the truth—that she feared for their lives. She'd seen his kind before and knew he wouldn't give up until someone was hurt or *dead.*

Chapter Four

Tara excused herself from Jodie and her friends to use the restroom. The restroom was small and cramped, but the seclusion from the rest of the group calmed her nerves somewhat. She still hadn't gotten over the earlier incident. She couldn't believe she'd let Jodie talk her into coming to Chester's Pool Hall after all that had happened.

She stared at the disheartening image in the mirror and shrugged. She didn't care how she looked anymore. The bruises were the least of her worries. She splashed cool water onto her face and patted it dry. She suddenly had an overwhelming sense of insecurity. She couldn't believe a week ago she was the happiest teenager alive without a fear in the world. Her biggest concern had been wearing the same dress as another girl to the spring fling. And now her parents were dead, and she didn't even know if she'd make it back to Tommy's apartment in one piece. She wrung her hands together. "Why me, God?" It felt like someone had taken her heart out and trampled all over it, and then shoved it back in, smashed.

Tara inhaled a deep breath and stepped away from the mirror. She couldn't fall apart in here. Jodie would think she was pathetic.

She dried her eyes with a paper towel and smiled at the mirror to see if the image would hide her pain. She had to go back out there and pretend she was just as tough as Jodie—like she was handling her parents' death, her attempted rape last night, and her near assault today with no problem. "Damn," she muttered, "how much can a person take?" She glanced toward the ceiling. "God, give me strength."

She cleared her throat, opened the door, and found her way back to the table.

The three guys sitting with them weren't ones she would normally choose to associate with, but they were acquaintances of Jodie, so they must be halfway trustworthy. Although, the way the Harley dude kept staring at her gave her the creeps. He dressed as if he were truly a Harley fan, too. He wore a black vest with the word *Harley* displayed across the back, black leather boots, and a black Harley bandanna tied around his long thinning brown hair. And to emphasize his character even more—his name was Bronze. Tara could almost bet that it wasn't his real name—he probably created it himself. The spider web wrinkles around his eyes and corners of his month led Tara to believe that he was over thirty.

Although the other two guys, Randy and Matt, were dressed more casual in jeans and tank tops, they were still more bizarre than what Tara was used to seeing. Randy wore his dark hair spiked with the tips bleached blond. He wore earrings everywhere imaginable, including his tongue, and colorful tattoos covered every inch of his arms.

Matt, on the other hand, wore his red afro *big*. She'd never seen so much hair on a guy before and it was as thick as it was red. His bright green tank top not only exposed his pale skin and hundreds of freckles but revealed how bony his arms were too.

Tara didn't think any of them had come to the bar together—playing pool was probably all they had in common.

"Left corner pocket." Jodie indicated which pocket by tapping her pool stick above it.

"Damn, Flipper, give me a break." Matt grunted and threw his hands up in the air as Jodie hit the eight ball in the hole. "I give up."

Jodie smiled and lifted her pool stick above her head. "Any one else care to step up to the table?"

Bronze laughed. "Thanks, but no thanks. Getting beat by a girl once a day is enough for me!"

33

"How bout it, Tara? Why don't you show her how to play?" Randy held the pool stick out.

"Me? You have to be kidding. I'm still trying to figure out what *Flipper* has to do with the game."

Jodie laughed so hard she snorted which caused more laughter from the table.

"We don't call her Flipper because of her pool skills." Matt pointed to the pinball table across the room. "See that machine? Jodie has the highest score on it. Before she started beating our asses at pool, she beat our asses at pinball."

"What can I say, I don't like to lose." Jodie lit the cigarette that was dangling between her lips.

"Wow, I feel stupid." Tara wondered just how long Jodie had been hanging around the joint, and if these were the only friends that she had.

"Hey, Flipper, you want to take a ride with me over to Queens? Remember, last time we saw your sister." Randy downed his mug of beer and stood.

Tara didn't miss the gleam in Jodie's eyes with the mentioning of her sister. She wasn't even aware that she had a sister.

Jodie glanced at Tara then back at Randy. "I don't know, Ran. You know I don't like to get involved with your dealings."

"Hey, just like last time. You go do your thing, and I'll do mine. We'll catch back up with each other—piece of cake."

Bronze stood and tossed some quarters on the table. "Come on, Matt, let's play a game." He poked his finger into Randy's chest. "Don't be getting Flipper in any kind of trouble, or I'll come and hunt you down."

Randy knocked Bronze's hand away. "Chill—she'll be fine."

"I don't know." Jodie nodded toward Tara. "I came with her."

Bronze's gaze narrowed as his eyes shifted to Tara. "She can stay here. I can give her a ride home on the bike."

Tara hoped Bronze didn't see her cringe. There was no way in hell she was getting on any bike with him. "That's okay, I can walk home." *If I remember how to get there,* she thought silently.

"Are you kidding? I'm not going to desert you and have you walking the streets with that lunatic out there!" Jodie paused. "Why don't you go with us?" She elbowed Randy. "You don't mind, do you?"

"Of course not. Any friend of yours is a friend of mine!"

Tara glanced at her watch. It was after seven. "Wow, I didn't know it was this late already. My uncle will be getting off in a couple of hours. I really should be home when he gets there."

"Come on, please?" Jodie puckered out her bottom lip and pretended to pout. "We can call him on Randy's cell phone later and let him know you're okay. Besides, it's Saturday night. What else do you have to do?"

"Well, I don't know…I guess my uncle won't care as long as I call him." Tara knew there was no way of talking her way out of this one. Besides, it did sound exciting to see more of the city. She'd been to New York a few times with her mother to shop at Soho and dine out, and her parents took her a couple of times to Central Park when she was younger. She'd still only seen a small portion of the city though. She knew there was a lot more to see.

Tara told Matt and Bronze goodbye. Bronze wouldn't let her leave until she promised she'd come back again with Jodie. She wondered how the guy could be attracted to her when she looked like a monster. None of them ever asked what happened—Jodie probably told them while she was in the restroom.

Jodie insisted that Tara sat in the front seat during the drive, although Tara would have preferred to sit in the back. She felt uncomfortable trying to make conversation with Randy. He wasn't much of a talker, and the only thing she could think to comment on was the weather and the size of the city. And Jodie didn't contribute any to the conversation; she was exceptionally quiet.

Tara clutched the armrest as Randy sped around another corner. The faster he drove, the more she regretted her decision to tag along. She recalled Jodie commenting that she didn't want to get involved in Randy's dealings. Tara wondered if he was up to something illegal. She suddenly had a sinking feeling—if Randy was busted for drugs or another serious act, she'd be an

35

accessory to the crime. She glanced in the backseat at Jodie—she was trying to light a cigarette, but the wind kept blowing the lighter out.

Tara quickly rolled up her window. "Sorry about that."

"That's okay."

Tara stared back out the passenger window as her doubts increased. She really didn't know Jodie. She'd only met her yesterday, and just because she'd saved her life didn't mean that her lifestyle was acceptable—she hung out at a pool hall and carried a gun—just like Stephanie Naylor, a rebellious girl in a recent novel that she'd read. Tara wouldn't be caught associating with a girl like Jodie back in her school. But she wasn't back in her high school anymore, and Jodie happened to be the only friend she had right now. Tara blinked back tears.

She was suddenly ashamed of the person she'd become. She knew if she would have had her other friends around she would have chose not to hang out with Jodie today. She couldn't believe she was so shallow after Jodie had risked her own life to save her. Tara tried to recall some of the scriptures from the past summers at church camp and realized she needed a refresher course on how everyone was equal. She glanced up toward the fresh stars in the sky and wondered if she'd ever get to go to church camp again. Her past life seemed so far away now.

After a while, Randy turned down a colorful strip with nightclubs. Neon lights flashed around the border of some of the windows, while well-endowed poster board girls lit up many of the others. Tara stared in disbelief at the crowd of people roaming the sidewalks. She cracked her window as loud music blared from the joints. Many young girls were dressed in mini skirts and halters, while some were dressed fancier in pantyhose and high heels, and they all seemed to be wearing lots of jewelry and make up. She glanced down at her own faded blue jeans and t-shirt and wondered if she was underdressed. She glanced toward the end of the block; a young gal in white shorts and knee-high white boots was leaning inside a car window. Tara guessed the girl to be close to her own age. "Are those hookers?"

Tara hadn't even realized she'd spoken aloud. It suddenly made sense why the girls were dressed the way they were.

"Yeah, they're everywhere!" Randy pulled down a nearby alley.

Tara glanced over her shoulder at Jodie. She had no idea this was where they were going. "I've never seen a hooker before."

"I'm related to one...*my sister*," Jodie said.

Randy parked the car. "Wait here a second while I check something out." He tucked an envelope into his shirt pocket and slipped out of the car.

"I'm sorry." Tara blushed. "I didn't mean anything by it. I just never saw one before." She suddenly wished she were back at Tommy's place. At least she felt safe locked in his apartment.

An elderly, gray haired man and a younger nice-looking black guy stepped outside the back door of one of the clubs. The elderly man was yelling at the other guy, something about if he done it one more time he was going to fire him. The black man continued to argue that it wasn't his fault. Tara shivered and glanced up and down the dark alley. She hoped Jodie didn't expect her to get out of the car.

"I need to talk to Nicole. I fear for her life...I want her to come home." Jodie rolled down her window and flicked her cigarette out.

Randy opened the car door and stuck his head in. "Okay ladies, meet me back here in an hour."

Jodie quickly scrambled out of the four-door Cavalier and stood waiting for Tara.

Tara hesitated and then climbed out. She wondered if Jodie noticed how uneasy she was. She wasn't accustomed to this kind of city life. Her parents would never allow her to go anywhere near the nightlife—they knew of the partying that teenagers were capable of. Tara's weekends were mostly filled with hanging out at friends' houses or going to the mall.

"We need to stick together." Jodie led the way down the murky alley.

Does she really think I'm going to do any different? Tara thought silently.

37

"Nicole has long reddish hair, but she usually wears it piled on top of her head. She's an inch taller than me, five foot ten." Jodie smiled. "I know…a Hispanic girl with red hair is unusual—she dyed it. It'll make her easier to spot."

"She sounds really pretty."

Jodie bowed her head. "I used to admire her..."

Tara kept her eyes alert as the dark settled in around her. Although the alley was wider than usual, she knew how easy it would be for someone to be lurking in the shadows of the buildings just like the thug had done last night. As they neared the end of the alley, she could hear the traffic and music, and she actually looked forward to being near the crowd, regardless of what they were doing. Anything was better than being in this dark alley. "Why is your sister doing this?"

A silver Impala suddenly sped up the alley and came to a halt just as a blond girl in a black leather mini skirt and white tank top rounded the corner. A man in a navy pinstriped suit jumped out of the car, rushed around the front of it, and carefully opened the passenger door. The girl climbed in, the man rushed back to the driver's side, and the car zoomed off. Tara thought the man was old enough to be the girl's father. She wondered if the man had a daughter of his own.

Tara sighed with relief as she stepped onto the pavement in front of the clubs.

"She chose this life because she thought it would be better than living with my mom." Jodie nodded to the entrance of the first club. "I usually don't go in. I just walk up and down the streets. Sometimes I get lucky and see her, and other times I don't."

"Life with your mom couldn't have been this bad." Tara grimaced as a drunk staggered into her, purposely touching her bottom as he passed.

Jodie suddenly stopped. "You have no clue! Nicole's life was pure hell with my mom. My mom almost killed her several times—on purpose."

"Wow!" Tara paused. "What about you? Is she violent toward you?"

"Yeah, but not near as bad as she was with Nicole." Jodie scanned the teenage girls while wandering up and down the streets. "My mom continuously picked on her. Every time she got drunk she'd start a fight with Nicole."

Tara couldn't imagine having a mom that was so heartless. She'd read the horror stories about mothers like Jodie's mom, but she never really thought much about it—probably, because her own life was so comfortable.

They walked up and down the congested sidewalks for the next forty minutes.

"I don't think we're going to have any luck tonight." Jodie stopped to squash her cigarette butt out. She scanned the surrounding area. "Wait…over there. That's her—coming out of that club. She's talking to that bald guy. Come on."

Nicole was heading in the opposite direction that they were.

Jodie jogged through the traffic and Tara followed.

"Nicole, wait up," Jodie called out.

Nicole whirled around. "Jodie, what are you doing here? I told you not to come here." She spun back around toward the gentleman. "Can you excuse me for just a second?" She glared at Jodie. "Go home, now."

"No! Come with me, Nicole…we'll get a place together…I'll get a job…" Jodie flicked a tear off her cheek.

"Don't do this. You know I can't go back now." She lowered her voice. "It's too late—I'm in too deep." She glanced nervously up and down the street. "I need to get to work."

"You don't have to do this! I'll help you," Jodie pleaded.

Tara felt like a third wheel listening in on their personal conversation. She thought about stepping away and gawking into a nightclub window. But the thought of being alone even for a few seconds terrified her.

"Jodie, I miss you and love you, but you don't understand how much trouble I'd be in if I try to leave J.J. Besides, he's been good to me. He's done more for me than mom ever did." Nicole pushed the auburn tresses off her forehead.

Tara couldn't peel her eyes off of Nicole. She thought she was the prettiest girl she'd ever seen. Her perfectly oval shaped face had a smooth, natural tan complexion. Girls back in her old school would lie in a tanning bed for months to obtain the same tan. And her hair was amazing—it had been curled and gathered up on top of her head. A gold barrette secured some of the locks, while the rest of the curls fell loosely around her face. Her big brown eyes shimmered under plum eye shadow and neatly plucked eyebrows. Her lips were shaded with cinnamon color lipstick. She wore tight black shorts and a white see-through button-down blouse, which revealed a lot of cleavage. Her high-heeled sandals added a couple of more inches to her long, lean body. Tara thought she'd make a perfect runway model.

The man whistled impatiently, and Nicole spun around, annoyed. "Just a sec, please." She turned back around toward Jodie. "I got to go. You doing okay with mom?"

Jodie rolled her eyes. "Yeah, she's still a bitch, though."

Nicole wrapped her arms around Jodie and squeezed her. "Hang in there, sis. She always liked you more." She held Jodie at arms length. "Please, don't follow in my footsteps. You're going to be something special one day—I just know you are."

"You can too. It's not too late."

"It is for me! I have to go now. Go home!" Nicole quickly spun around before Jodie could protest. She slid her arm through the guy's arm and hurried down the street.

Jodie stood silently for several minutes staring after Nicole

Tara waited until Nicole had blended into the crowd before she spoke. "Are you okay?" Jodie didn't answer. "We should be going… Randy will be waiting. I probably need to call my uncle, too."

Jodie shrugged. "I'm sorry. Sure, let's go." With her head bowed, she led the way down the street, stopping at the corner to wait for the traffic to clear.

A white mustang pulled up next to the curb, and a heavy-set man in his mid forty's leaned across the seat and winked at Jodie. "How much, honey?"

Tara's jaw dropped as Jodie approach the car.

Jodie thrust her leg forward and rested her hands on her hips. "Well, what do you think I'm worth, big boy?"

Tara couldn't believe her ears. She'd just scolded Nicole for the very same thing. Was this her way at getting back at Nicole? Surely, she wasn't thinking clearly. "We need to go, Jodie."

"Just a second. I want to know how much this handsome fellow thinks I'm worth."

"How about sixty?" The man's eyebrows furrowed as he waited for Jodie's reply.

"Sixty? That's all I'm worth to you?" Jodie casually pushed her shirt down off her shoulder. "Are you sure?"

"Hey, I can go on down the block and get it for fifty," the man said flatly.

"For your information, mister, I'm not no whore!" Jodie shrieked. "And if I give the police your license plate number and let them know you tried to pick up on a minor, they will easily be able to identify you. And I will take even more pleasure in calling your wife and letting her know how you like to spend your Saturday nights."

"You slut!" The man rolled up the passenger window and peeled out.

Jodie doubled over, laughing.

"I can't believe you just did that." Tara stared after the car for several seconds. Suddenly she giggled. "Did you see the look on his face? How did you know he was married?"

"His wedding ring was lying in the ashtray." Jodie caught her breath and led the way across the street. "I'm sorry, but I couldn't resist."

"I wasn't sure what you were up to. Do you do that often?"

"I've done it a few times. All these married scumbags slumming around make me sick."

Tara was glad the incident took Jodie's mind off her sister.

They reached the alley, and Tara slid closer to Jodie. The alley seemed quieter than before. The memory of the night before came rushing back, and goose bumps spiked her arms. She strained to see Randy's car. It was parked in the same spot he'd left it, but she didn't see him anywhere nearby.

41

They reached the car, and Tara quickly glanced through the window. She was relieved to see Randy sitting behind the steering wheel, drumming his thumbs against it.

He glanced up and hurriedly unlocked the car. "I'm glad you gals made it—we need to get out of here."

"Something wrong?" Jodie asked.

"Nothing I can't handle. We just need to go." He pushed the button to lock the doors as soon as the girls were in and shifted the gear into drive.

Tara thought it was strange that he didn't turn his headlights on until they were out of the alley. She didn't know what it was about, but she was glad to get out of the vicinity. She was actually looking forward to going back to Tommy's place. She decided not to call her uncle. She'd explain everything once she got home. It felt odd referring to Tommy's place as home. She missed her old bedroom and all the stuffed animals she'd pile on her bed every morning after she made it.

She had to find a way to quit thinking about the past. She shifted her gaze to Randy's arms, cleared her throat, and asked about his tattoos. She was a little more relaxed with him now than she was earlier. She imagined it was because she was so relieved to be going home. It had been another long day, and she was worn out.

After several miles, Randy pulled up in front of Jodie's building. "See you ladies at Chester's soon."

"Okay—thanks, Ran." Jodie climbed out.

"Yeah, thanks," Tara added.

Randy waved and pulled away from the curb.

Jodie glanced up toward her building. "Damn, I forgot to go by Maddie's."

"Who?"

"A little old woman that lives in my building, who means a lot to me. I'll have to introduce you sometime." She gestured toward Tara's building. "Come on, I'll walk you to your door."

"You don't have to. I don't want you to have to walk back by yourself." Tara glanced nervously toward the carload of boys at the end of the block.

Jodie gave Tara a little shove to indicate she wasn't taking no for an answer. "Yeah, but I have my own personal bodyguard, remember."

They hurried up the stairs and inside Tara's building.

"You want to come in and meet my uncle?" Tara twisted the key in the lock.

"Maybe another time. I'm really hungry, so I'll see you soon." Jodie spun around and jogged down the hall.

Tara watched as Jodie left the building. She wondered what was worse, not having a mother at all or having a mother like Jodie's. She decided not having one would be better.

She pushed the door open and froze. Tommy stood in the midst of overturned furniture, broken glass, and scattered books. The wooden stand the TV had set on was broken, and the TV was gone. The cabin doors in the kitchen were open, and broken dishes were strewn from one end to the other. Tomatoes from the refrigerator were smashed all over the kitchen floor.

Snake! Tara was sure it had been him. The hair on her arms stiffened as though she'd been struck by lightening. An intense knot formed in the pit of her stomach. Her eyes welled up as she fell to her knees. "Oh God, Tommy," she cried. "He's going to kill me!"

Chapter Five

Jodie walked Tara to her first hour English class. "I'll meet you out front after school." She noticed Tara was chewing on her nails again. Tommy had gone inside the office with her to enroll but had left shortly afterwards, leaving Tara to fend for herself.

"Okay, see you later," Tara hesitated before stepping into the classroom.

Jodie waved and spun back toward the way she'd come. She'd forgotten an assignment in her locker. If she hurried, she could make it to her class before the final bell rang.

She couldn't believe the weekend was already over. She'd spent all day Sunday helping Tara and her uncle clean up their apartment. Tara was certain that Snake had done the damage, but Jodie wasn't convinced yet. She thought that it would be an awful daring move if he had. *How could he be certain that Tara wasn't going to press charges for the early incident?* It just didn't make sense…unless he wasn't very smart, or *he just wasn't scared.* Jodie shivered at the thought as she pulled her locker open. She grabbed the notebook she needed and slammed the door.

She hurried down the hall, keeping her head bowed as she passed some girls who belong to a gang known as the Angels. She knew better than to make eye contact with any of them. She didn't want to be accused of challenging them—they were always looking for an excuse to fight.

She slipped through the door of Mr. Gullivan's Geography class just as the bell rung. She made her way to the back of the room where she usually sat. Taylor smiled and moved her purse out of the seat she was saving for her.

Jodie had never spent any time with Taylor except for the one hour each day in Geography. Taylor didn't say much, but when she did it was always something nice. If Jodie received a good mark on a test, she always had a positive comment to make. Jodie found herself trying harder in Mr. Gullivan's class than in all her others. She knew it was because of Taylor's compliments. She'd praised Jodie more in one day than her mother had her whole life.

Jodie tried to focus her attention on Mr. Gullivan's discussion on South America, but her mind kept drifting to Nicole. She couldn't understand why Nicole wouldn't come home with her. They could get jobs and rent an apartment together. Jodie had thought it all through. She'd even quit school if it got Nicole off the streets. She could always go back later.

Taylor slid a stick of gum on Jodie's desk, and Jodie nodded thanks. Besides Maddie, Taylor had to be the nicest colored girl that she'd ever met. She wondered briefly about Taylor's social life. Jodie was certain she wasn't mixed up with any gangs. She was too well mannered—a classic girl with a tall, lean figure. She wore colored ribbons twisted around the multiple braids in her hair. The colors in her shirt blended with the ribbons, and her fingernails were neatly filed and polished to match. She decided Taylor led a comfortable life.

Jodie turned her attention toward Mr. Gullivan's question. He called on Carlos who was sitting two seats in front of her. He shrugged and bowed his head. His lengthy wavy black hair fell to the sides of his face. Her stomach did the usual summersault as she wondered what it would be like to go out with the hot Latin dude. He'd flirted with her a few times in between classes, but it had never led to anything.

She scooted down in her chair as Mr. Gullivan scanned the students, searching for another victim. Although Jodie knew most the answers, she never volunteered. She hated speaking out in class—everyone always turned to stare. And if she heard whispering or snickering, she'd assume someone was talking about her.

After awhile Mr. Gullivan stopped calling on the students and went back to lecturing. Jodie's mind drifted, as Mr. Gullivan's words grew monotonous.

The bell finally rung and Jodie snatched up her book. She told Taylor she'd see her tomorrow and hurried toward the door.

Carlos slipped up beside her as she entered the hall. "Hey, slow down. Are you that anxious to get to your next class?"

Jodie grinned. "Hey—sorry. I have to go all the way across the school, and you know how much time they give us."

"So don't go!"

"What?"

Carlos winked. "Let's go do something fun and adventurous."

Jodie hesitated. She couldn't tell if he was serious or joking. "I can't—I have a test next hour."

"I see how you are. Okay, what about Friday night? You want to hang out—I know a kickin' party that's happening."

"Sure," Jodie said without thinking.

"Should we meet somewhere, or you want me to come by?"

"Umm…we'd probably better meet," She said quickly. She knew if he met her mom that would be the last date she ever had with him. "Are you familiar with Chester's Pool Hall?"

"I've never hung out at the red-neck joint, but I know where it is," he teased. "I'll be waiting for you—outside that is—at nine."

"Okay, see you later." She turned toward the opposite hall.

Carlos whistled. "You're looking fine, Jodie girl."

Jodie blushed as she glanced over her shoulder. She was sure everyone in the halls had heard, although she couldn't deny the warm fuzzy feeling he'd created in the pit of her stomach.

As hard as she tried to concentrate in all of her other classes, her mind kept drifting to Carlos. She visualized him on a beach with his dark tan skin and rippling muscles wearing only a pair of skimpy swim trunks. They would hold hands and walk on the shoreline as the waves splashed over their feet. He'd turned to

46

kiss her as the sun was setting, and his dark dreaming eyes would sparkle as he called her *Jodie girl.* She'd run her fingers through his silky jet-black hair.

Jodie quickly drifted back to reality as the final bell of the day rung. She knew she was living in a dream world, and none of it would ever come true. She was surprised Carlos wanted to hang out with her at all. There were far prettier girls in the school. Perhaps he thought she was easy. She suddenly wished she'd made up an excuse not to go. What was she thinking? She didn't even particularly like going to parties. Everyone always ended up drunk and fighting.

She slammed her locker shut and headed toward the front of the school. She'd almost forgotten that she was supposed to meet Tara. She wasn't used to having friends. *And she liked it that way!*

She immediately regretted her negative attitude. It wasn't Tara's fault that her life was so screwed up. Jodie could easily relate to her unfortunate circumstances.

She exited the school and scanned the crowd. She spotted Tara with her head bowed, leaning against the flagpole. Jodie hurried toward her. "Hey, we got to hurry if we want to catch the bus, or we'll have a long walk."

"Sure." Tara followed Jodie to the bus.

Jodie grabbed the first vacant seat and scooted toward the window. "Well, how was your first day?"

Tara's eyes clouded over. "I hate this school," she said softly.

Jodie should have known it wouldn't be any treat. "If it's the kids you're worried about just ignore them!"

"I can ignore the comments made about me, but the mama jokes really hit a nerve, and it's so immature!"

"You can't let them get under your skin, or they will taunt you even more. You'll have to learn to shut them out. If you don't, it will just keep eating at you. It's the only way you'll survive at this school."

"Oh God, Jodie, how do you do it? I'll never make it here!"

"You will—just take one day at a time."

47

Tara grew silent, and Jodie figured she just needed time to adjust. She'd gone through a lot in the last few days. She was glad that Tara's uncle had changed the locks on their apartment door—maybe Tara would feel a little safer.

The bus dropped them off five blocks away from their street. Jodie scanned the area to see if Snake was lurking anywhere nearby. She sighed, relieved that she didn't see him. She'd been worried all day, especially since she had to leave her pistol at home. "I don't see him anywhere."

Tara's eyes darted wildly up and down the street as she slid closer to Jodie.

Jodi suddenly had an idea. She'd take Tara to meet Maddie. She was certain that was just what Tara needed. Maddie had a magical way of lifting spirits.

"Hey, let's stop by Maddie's place. You'll like her."

Tara grimaced. "I don't know. I don't think I'd be very good company today."

Jodie led the way home. "Come on." She didn't wait for a reply. She marched up the stairs toward the lobby door. She glanced over her shoulder at Tara. "You coming?"

Silently, Tara trudged up the stairs and followed Jodie into the building.

Jodie knocked on Maddie's door, and after a few minutes, Maddie peeked through the peephole.

She immediately opened the door and peered over the rim of her glasses. "You okay, Jodanne?" She stared curiously at Tara.

"I'm fine. I just wanted you to meet a friend. Her castle is across the street." She smiled and nodded toward Tara. "This is Tara Woodward."

"Oh…well, hello Tara."

"Hello, nice to meet you."

Maddie opened the door wider. "Come on in. I just took an apple pie out of the oven, and I think I have a half gallon of vanilla ice cream in the freezer."

Jodie and Tara followed Maddie into the small cluttered kitchen.

Jodie's stomach rumbled as she sniffed the aroma. "Wow that smells so good. Are you sure you have enough, Maddie?"

"Child, do I look like I can eat a whole apple pie by myself?"

Jodie giggled and Tara joined in.

Maddie pulled out chairs around the table for the girls to sit, and then reached for the saucers in the cupboard. "So, Tara, how long have you been in the neighborhood?"

"Not quite a week. I'm living with my uncle." She hesitated. "My parents were killed in an auto accident."

Maddie's smile suddenly faded. "Oh my. You poor thing." She scooped up a dip of ice cream and dropped it on a slice of pie. She pushed the dish toward Tara. "I know it's hard losing your loved ones. I also had to bury my son. It was the hardest thing I ever had to do. But rest your heart; they are in a much better place than we are." She pushed a plate toward Jodie. "Did Jodie warn you about the neighborhood? Unfortunately, it's not the safest place to live."

"Yeah, Tara's already found that out." Jodie shoved a bite in her mouth and moaned. "Ah, this is so good."

"Yes, it is. Thank you very much Mrs...." Tara stuttered.

"You can call me Maddie." She poured the girls a glass of lemonade. "How about a game of gin rummy?"

Jodie grinned secretively at Maddie. "That sounds fun. Is that okay, Tara?"

"Sure."

"You don't get mad when you lose, do you?" Maddie asked seriously, but then grinned and winked at Tara.

Tara giggled. "Not usually."

They ate their pie and ice cream while they joked and played cards.

After an hour and another loss, Jodie tossed her cards on the table. "I'm sorry gals, but as much as I'd like to stick around to get beat again—I can't. I have to get home and clean the kitchen before my mom gets home."

Maddie stood. "Everything going okay at home? Did Nicole ever come back?"

"Not yet. But I'm still hopeful."

49

Maddie walked the girls to the door. "You girls come back again, and maybe I'll let you win a game next time."

Tara grinned. "Okay, thanks."

Jodie nudged Tara. "Don't get your hopes up. She's never let me win a game in my life." She shook her finger at Maddie "One of these days I'm going to win."

Maddie winked. "Sure you will, girl."

They told Maddie bye, and Jodie walked Tara outside. "I'll see you in the morning. You sure you don't want me to walk you to your apartment?"

"I'm sure—I'll be fine. Thanks, though."

Jodie waited until Tara had gone inside her building, and then she hurried toward her own apartment.

She inserted the key and froze. The door was already unlocked. Her mother seldom left the bar this early in the afternoon.

A thousand images rushed through her head: the physical attack on Tara, Snake's threatening voice, the break-in at Tommy's. Maybe it was Snake, and now he'd found Jodie's pad. "Damn," she swore under her breath as she realized her gun was inside under the mattress.

She slowly pushed the door open and stepped inside the front room. Her eyes darted to every corner of the room. Her empty milk glass still set on the end table, the crumpled up piece of paper she'd tossed on the couch this morning remained untouched. Everything looked the same as it did when she'd left for school. She thrust her ear forward, listening, as she took another step.

Jodie slowly entered into the kitchen, and while keeping her eyes glued to the hallway she quietly pulled out the silverware drawer. Her fingers fumbled over the forks and butter knifes until she felt the tip of a butcher knife. She retrieved the knife and left the drawer open.

She wiped the sweat off her forehead with the back of her hand and made her way down the hallway. Her mother's bedroom was first—the door was open. The bedcovers had been tossed to the floor, and clothes spewed out across the bed but, this was common. Her mother never cleaned. She usually slept in until noon or later and then would start her daily routine back down at Grover's Bar. She'd make her rounds until she ran out of money or couldn't stand up any longer. Sometimes she'd come home alone, and other times she'd pick up any guy that would have her.

Jodie glanced toward her room at the end of the hall and noticed the light shining from under the door. She was certain she'd turned it off before she'd left. Her adrenaline increased. She held the knife above her head and crept slowly down the hall. She stopped in front of the door and held her breath. She counted silently to three, kicked the door opened, and jumped into the room, ready to attack. But the room was empty. Although it wasn't ram-sacked, Jodie could tell someone had been there.

She hurried toward the closet and poked her head inside—no one was there.

She glanced around the room soaking in every little detail. She lifted her mattress and sighed—the pistol was still there. But the shirt that she'd discarded on the bed earlier was now tossed on the floor. Her pockets on her winter coat, which she'd hung on the back of a chair, were turned inside out, and some of her worn sneakers were pulled out of the closet. Her room was small and easily cluttered, so it was hard to tell if anything was missing. But something was wrong; she could feel it in her bones. She rummaged through her drawers and found everything intact. She studied the top of her dresser and sorted through her makeup and the stacks of papers, but everything was in order. She scanned the room again, puzzled. It was unlike her mother to rummage through her room.

And then it hit her—she suddenly realized what was missing. "Son-of-a-bitch!" Jodie frantically searched behind the dresser. She fell to her knees and ran her hand underneath the dresser— nothing. "What the hell?" She stood and took one last glance across the dresser, knowing it wouldn't be there. The 5X7 picture frame with Nicole's picture was gone.

Chapter Six

The next few days weren't any better for Tara. It seemed like she had to tiptoe through the halls so she wouldn't draw attention to herself. She couldn't believe kids could be so rude. In her old school she'd been popular; she was the class secretary and a drum majorette. Here, she was nothing but a target for bullies and gang members.

She hated the school, the city, the fog in the mornings, the cramped apartment, and the rough neighborhood.

During classes, she'd daydream of her mom and dad and the wonderful life they'd had before the tragedy. At night, she'd lie awake for hours reliving the horrible nightmare from Snake's assault.

Fortunately, there hadn't been any mishaps with him since the day they'd run into him at Kingdom Hill. Although she was certain, he was responsible for breaking into their apartment! And Monday, someone broke into Jodie's apartment and snooped through her room, taking a picture of her sister. Tara knew it wasn't a coincidence. The hoodlum was up to no good.

Jodie had asked Tara to ride to Queens with her on Saturday to warn her sister about Snake. Tara didn't especially want to go back to the area, but it was the least she could do for her new friend.

She slammed her Algebra book shut and turned the TV on. She flipped through the basic channels and sighed. There wasn't anything worth watching. She knew she shouldn't complain, considering they didn't have a TV at all until a couple of days ago. Tommy had found a cheap 19" at a garage sale.

She glanced at the clock—it was just after six. Tommy was still at work and wouldn't be home for a couple more hours. She walked back to her Algebra book and flipped it back to the page of her homework. She stared blankly at the page for a few minutes and then slammed the book shut again. "I hate Algebra! I hate school!" She walked to the window and stared out. "I hate my life." Tears surfaced as she stared at the street below. All week she'd stayed locked up in the apartment, leaving only to go to school. Although it was already Thursday, and the week was nearly over, she didn't think she could stand another moment in the apartment. She grabbed her jacket off the back of the chair and headed for Jodie's place. Surely, she'd be safe long enough to walk across the street.

She'd only been to Jodie's apartment one other time. And it was only for a brief moment while Jodie had grabbed her purse. Her mother hadn't been at home.

Now as she stood outside Jodie's apartment she wondered if she'd made a mistake. She could hear a woman screaming and then what sounded like glass breaking. She thought about just going back home, but then she remembered how Jodie had risked her own life to save her.

Tara pounded on the door.

"What the hell do you want?" A shrewd woman's voice bellowed from behind the closed door.

Tara hesitated. "I was looking for Jodie."

The door flung open. "Yeah…and who are you?"

Tara tried not to stare at the ghastly woman—her eyes were blood shot, and her dark hair was ratty and falling out of her ponytail. The lady reeked of alcohol and looked mean as hell, although she was thin as a pancake. Tara had no doubt that it was Jodie's mother. "I'm Tara. I live across the street." She glanced past the woman to see if Jodie was nearby. She didn't see her, but shattered glass was scattered across the floor.

"I don't need any of Jodie's damn friends hanging around here eating all our food!" She rested her hands on her hips and

53

grunted. "I didn't even know she had friends!" She suddenly raised her voice, "Why the hell would you want a friend like her?"

"I…" Tara stuttered.

Jodie suddenly appeared in the hallway with a gym bag flung over her shoulder. Blood was dripping off her lower lip and her eye was swollen. "Leave her alone, Mom!"

"Where do you think your going, smart ass?"

"Away from you!" Jodie tried to slide by her mother, but her mom stuck her foot out and tripped her, and then laughed as Jodie hit the floor.

The woman's face suddenly turned somber. "You're such a fucking whore!"

Jodie jumped to her feet and rushed to the door. "Whatever!" She motioned Tara to follow.

Tara could hear Jodie's mother screaming as they scurried down the hallway.

Jodie reached the end of the hall, spun around, and flipped the bird toward the apartment. "Bitch," she mumbled.

Tara was thankful Jodie's mother had already slammed the door shut, or she might have stumbled down the hall after them. And after what she'd just witnessed, she believed the crazy woman was capable of anything. *Poor Jodie*, she thought. *What a horrible mother.*

"Are you okay?" Tara jogged down the stairs after Jodie.

"Yeah, I'm fine."

"Hey, slow down." Tara struggled for the right words to comfort her friend. "What are you going to do now? You want to come to my place?"

"Thanks, but I think I want to be alone." She jogged across the street and then called back over her shoulder. "I'll catch up with you later."

"I want to help you," Tara yelled.

Jodie didn't respond. She continued up the street.

Tara watched as Jodie rounded the corner toward the alley— the same alley that she was almost raped. "Where the heck are you going?" she mumbled to herself.

54

Tara crossed the street and rounded the corner, too. She knew Jodie needed help, and she wasn't about to leave her wandering the streets alone. She kept her eyes on Jodie from a distance. She'd seen her go toward an aged brick building. Tara quickly ducked behind an old car as Jodie spun around to see if she was being followed.

Tara edged closer. Puzzled, she watched as Jodie slid behind a bush. After several minutes, Tara slid up next to the bush. "Jodie," she whispered into the bush. She slowly bent some branches back to see if she could see her, but all she saw was a boarded up window. She ducked behind the bush and tapped on the boards. "Jodie, are you in there?"

Jodie pulled a board down. "You followed me!" She sighed and removed the rest of the boards. "Did anyone see you?"

"No, I don't think so."

"Well, hurry, get inside."

Tara lowered herself through the window and grunted as she hit the floor. She gazed around the tiny room. "Wow, what is this?"

"It's my secret pad, and you're to never tell anyone. Do you understand?"

"Yeah, sure. Do you actually stay here?"

"Sometimes. I can be left alone here unlike back there in that hellhole!"

"Jodie, I am so sorry you have to live like that. You want me to go get some ice for your eye and something for your lip?"

"No, I'm fine!" She wiped the blood from her lip with the sleeve of her shirt. "I bet you'll never stop by my house again."

Tara hesitated and glanced down at the floor. "Probably not."

"And she's not even completely toasted yet. By the time she finishes the bottle of whiskey she'll be a mess!"

"Can't you report her to someone?"

"And then what?" Jodie lit a cigarette. "Social Services would rip me out of the house so fast. I've heard the stories of kids in foster care. Most of the time, they end up in worse predicaments. Some of them are even raped." She blew smoke out and shrugged. "No thank you! I'll wait it out. At least my mom keeps food in the fridge."

"Wow, I'm sorry…I just didn't realize…" Tara was on the verge of tears. She'd been too wrapped up in her own problems to notice Jodie's troubles. "Where's your father?"

"I've never had one—neither did Nicole. My mom claims she can't remember, and I believe her. Both times were probably just one night stands." She sighed. "Oh, believe me, I got it pretty good compared to a lot of kids in the neighborhood. Hell, there're kids under twelve selling drugs just to support their own habits."

"That's so sad."

"Yeah, well, it's life in the 'hood. I'm just biding my time until I graduate."

"It's not fair. You shouldn't have to live like that." She thought of her own precious mother and fiddled with the ring on her finger that her mom once wore. "Is there anything I can do?"

Jodie flicked the ashes in the ashtray. "Nope, but thanks."

"Do you want to do something tomorrow night?"

"Sorry, but I've kind of already made plans?"

"Oh…" Tara glanced toward the floor. "Of course, you have other friends."

Jodie shook her head. "No, it's not like that." She squashed the cigarette out. "I guess I kind of have a date."

"I didn't think you had a boyfriend."

"He just asked me out this week."

"Oh, okay, what about Saturday? Are we still going to Queens?"

Jodie's eyes suddenly clouded over. "I have to! I know Snake's the one that broke in and took the picture. I'm so scared he's going to get to Nicole before I do."

"I don't think he'll be able to find her," Tara said, although she wasn't quite convinced herself. Snake seemed to be capable of anything.

"I hope you're right."

"Hey, I better go before it gets any later. I don't want to be in that alley any longer than I have to."

56

"Sure." Jodie stood. "I can walk you back."

"No, don't." She gestured for Jodie to stop. "I know you mean well, and I appreciate it, but I need to quit hiding behind you."

"But what if..."

Tara interrupted, "It's still light out—I'll be fine."

Jodie reached for her jacket, dug into the pocket, and tossed the can of mace to Tara. "At least take this. I don't need it anymore." She patted her jacket. "I have something better now!"

"Okay, thanks." She waited until Jodie removed the boards. "I'll see you in the morning."

"About tomorrow...I'm going to skip school. It's embarrassing to go with a busted lip and black eye—someone always has to make a friggen comment. But I'll see you Saturday."

"Okay. Have fun tomorrow night." She quietly slipped through the window.

Tara cautiously looked up and down the empty alley. She glanced toward the trash bin where Snake had dragged her. She shivered as the horrid images materialized again.

Suddenly, fear overwhelmed her—she clutched the mace in her hand and shot down the alley as fast as she could. She rounded the corner, relieved to see children playing ball, and other women still socializing outside. She jogged toward her building. Although she didn't think Snake would try anything in public, she'd never let her guard down again.

She bounded into the apartment, slamming the door behind her and locking it. Although she hated the cramped apartment— at least she was safe *for now*. She thought of Jodie. She couldn't imagine her sleeping in that hole all night. *How could a mother treat her own daughter so badly? And why does God take the good mothers?* She clinched her fists as she fought back tears. Every day was a challenge. She missed going to church and hanging out with her friends. She missed dinners with her parents, shopping with her mom, and playing catch with her dad.

She dropped down on the couch as the tears surfaced. She was certain she'd never be happy again. *Please God... don't leave me now,* she prayed.

***

Jodie woke to the early noises of the city. She pulled the blanket over her head just as a siren blared in the distance. "Shit," she mumbled and sat up. She patted her hair down with her hand and reached for a cigarette. She hadn't slept well, and her back was killing her. Her face felt like it had been ran over by a train. She pulled her mirror out of her bag to check the damage. The swelling wasn't bad, but the eye was bruised across the eyelid and beneath it. "Damn it!" How was she supposed to go on a date with Carlos, looking like she'd been in a gang fight?

She thought about not showing up but quickly shook off the notion. She was sure he'd never ask her out again if she did that. She'd just have to go like she was and make the best of it.

She checked the time; it was only 9:00 a.m., and she was sure her mom would still be asleep. Jodie struggled with what to do. Her stomach growled. She hadn't eaten since lunch yesterday. She slid her jacket on and flung her gym bag over her shoulder. She decided she'd stay at Maddie's until her mom left the apartment.

Jodie was glad Maddie was an early riser. She answered the door after only one knock.

"For crying out loud, child!" She touched Jodie's chin, tilting her head upwards. "What happened?"

"Mother again."

"Come inside." She slammed the door shut. "What is wrong with that woman? She needs her head examined!" She rested her hands on her hips. "It's the alcohol that triggers her meanest, you know. It's pure poison." She pulled a chair out at the kitchen table for Jodie to sit. "My husband was an alcoholic. Although he was never as violent as your mother, there were days when I wanted to pack my bags and leave."

"What stopped you?"

"Jerome. He was crazy about his dad, and John was equally as crazy about him." She reached for the orange juice in the refrigerator. "He took his anger out on me, but he'd never raise his voice to Jerome." She set a glass of juice in front of Jodie. "I'm making you some breakfast, so don't argue."

"No argument here," Jodie said.

Maddie dropped some bacon in a skillet and arranged it with a fork. "Jerome was only eight when his father passed away." She cracked two eggs in a different skillet. "It was his liver—all the drinking finally caught up with him. If he'd had some insight about Jerome's involvement in a gang, he would have quit drinking and stuck around to straighten him out!" Maddie's voice quivered, "And maybe Jerome would still be alive."

"I'm sorry, Maddie."

"Listen to me ramble on and on. What's done is done! We need to go forward—not backwards. You need to remember that, child." She stuck a piece of bread in the toaster. "You still have a bright future ahead of you! Don't let your upsets with your mother destroy your dreams." She scooped the bacon and eggs up on a plate. "You're a beautiful, smart young lady, and you can do anything you set your mind to."

"You always know how to cheer me up, Maddie." Jodie sniffed. "Oh, that smells wonderful."

Maddie reached for the toast and set the plate in front of Jodie. "Eat up. There's more if that's not enough."

"Oh, this is plenty. I haven't eaten since lunch yesterday!"

"Jodanne, haven't I told you before to come here and eat? This happened yesterday? Why didn't you come to me?" She shook her head. "You didn't stay in your hiding place all night, did you?"

Jodie had told Maddie about her secret spot and how sometimes she slept there. "I'm sorry, Maddie. I just needed to be alone."

"I worry about you out there on the streets."

"I know you do, and I'm sorry."

"You promise you'll come to me next time."

"I promise, Maddie." Jodie said, although she wasn't sure if she meant it.

After she'd finished eating, Maddie got out the cards and they played until after noon.

Jodie finally stood. "She should be gone by now. I'm going to go on home and shower. Thanks, Maddie, for everything!"

"You're welcome. Don't be a stranger."

"I won't."

Jodie hurried toward her apartment. She was eager to have the place to herself for a few hours. But her excitement suddenly vanished as she stared at the black paint scribbled across her apartment door: *K Fucking Sister Bitch!*

Chapter Seven

After several trips to Chester's Pool Hall, Jodie finally gave up on trying to locate Randy. She'd hoped that she'd find him and hitch a ride to Queens. She was worried sick about Nicole and didn't want to wait until tomorrow. But it looked like she wasn't going to have a choice.

She was certain Snake had painted her door. Luckily, it was fresh paint, and Jodie easily removed it before her mother saw it. Not that her mother would be worried about Nicole but more upset about the paint on the door.

Jodie debated whether to meet with Carlos. She wasn't in any mood to socialize but finally decided keeping busy might keep her mind from imagining the worst. She figured she might as well stay up all night because she knew sleep wouldn't come easy.

It was a quarter till nine when she finally returned to Chester's. She'd spent the last two hours stealing whiskey and selling to some eager minors. It had turned into a more difficult task than it usually was. Buck, the manager of Conner Liquors, kept his eyes on Jodie the whole time. Only while he was ringing up a purchase for another customer was she able to slip some bottles in her jacket. After paying for a bottle of pop, she'd half expected him to frisk her, but a few hoodlums entered the store and his attention shifted to them.

She was going to have to get a job soon—she couldn't risk going to jail. She'd never finish school then.

Jodie made one last trip through the pool hall to see if Randy was there, but only Bronze was leaning over the pool table. "Hey Bronze, you seen Ran?"

"Not today, Flip. What's up? You want to play next?"

"No, not tonight. If Randy comes in will you give him a message?"

"Sure." He lined his pool stick up, closed one eye, slid the stick back and forth, and then made his shot, sending the white ball into the side pocket. "Shit."

"It's all about patience." Jodie grinned.

Bronze rolled his eyes. "Thanks Flip! Hurry with that message before you jinx me!"

"Tell Randy to make sure and not leave without me tomorrow. I'll be here around six." She paused. "Is that too much for you to remember?"

"Well, you're fired up tonight, aren't you?" He cocked his head sideways. "I got you covered. Now take that smart mouth of yours and get out of here before you make me lose." He leaned over the table to line up another shot.

"Okay, one more thing." She shook her head. "Don't take that shot—you won't make it. Try this one." She pointed to the red solid ball. "Right here." She tapped on the left corner pocket.

"You know what really pisses me off is that you're probably right." He hesitated and then did what Jodie suggested. The red ball rolled to the left corner pocket and dropped. "Well, what do you know!" He threw his hands up in the air.

"See—told you. Don't forget to tell Randy."

Jodie slipped outside to wait for Carlos. She chose the wooden bench next to the front door, so she wouldn't miss Randy if he showed up.

She'd only been waiting ten minutes when she spotted Carlos rounding the corner in tight blue jeans and a black T-shirt. His dark wavy hair was pulled back into a ponytail and a gold hoop hung from his left ear. The muscles in Jodie's stomach tightened as he neared. His smile was suggestively flirty, and his dark magnetic eyes made her heart skip a beat.

"Hey, Jodie girl, what's happening?"

"Not much." She stood.

"Ouch, what happened to your eye? Did you get in a fight in that redneck joint?"

"Nope. My mother and I don't always see eye to eye." She pointed to her eye. "Get it?" She grinned. "And it's not a redneck joint, either!"

"That explains why you weren't at school today!" He nodded toward the pool hall. "And that *is* a redneck joint."

"Yeah… and where do you hang out?"

"Well, since you asked, I'll show you." He grabbed her hand and led her to the crosswalk.

She figured he'd let go of her hand after they crossed the street, but he continued to hold on. She hoped he didn't notice her occasional glances over her shoulder. She hadn't brought her pistol with her, and Snake was still fresh on her mind.

After a few blocks, they stopped in front of a red brick building. Flashing blue lights bordered a sign that read Snyder's Pub and Grill. Vintage beer signs decorated the large window. Carlos opened the door and bowed. "This is the coolest place on this strip."

Jodie stepped into the lobby. It was definitely roomy and buzzing with people. It wasn't a classic restaurant but comfortably casual. Chatter could be heard in every direction and smoke lingered in the air.

Carlos led her to a booth. "This is where I spend most of my evenings."

Jodie's eyebrows furrowed. "You do?" It was hip, but she couldn't imagine Carlos hanging out there. The guys sitting at the bar didn't seem his type. They were older men, ripping jokes and sipping margaritas, while Carlos seemed like a slam-it-down beer-type dude.

Carlos waved to a middle-aged waitress as he slid into the booth "I work here. My uncle owns the place."

"Oh, I see." Now it made sense to her. She glanced toward the wall decorated cleverly with vintage beer cans. "Is your uncle here?"

"No, but he owes me a favor, so dinner is on him tonight. He frowns at me for drinking beer, but he never objects." He turned toward the slightly plump waitress approaching the table, "Hey Francie, how about hooking us up with a couple of cold Budweisers?" He glanced back at Jodie. "You do like beer?"

Jodie nodded.

Francie shook her head. "Louie wouldn't approve, you know. If inspectors come in here…"

Carlos interrupted, "I have an I.D." He winked. "The picture might look a little different, but it will do."

"I have an I.D., too," Jodie blurted. She lowered her eyes to the menu as the lady eyed her suspiciously.

"See, Fran baby, there's nothing to worry about."

The waitress blushed and giggled. "Well, I guess since you're his beloved nephew and his favorite employee I have no choice." Her smile faded as her eyes met Jodie's. "But how do we know she can be trusted?"

Carlos laughed. "You're kidding, right? You think she's an undercover inspector or something?"

She rolled her eyes. "Of course not. I was just joking. I'll be right back with those brews." She ducked around the corner.

"Wow, I don't think she likes me much," Jodie whispered. She was certain the woman had a thing for Carlos, although she had to be over forty years old.

"Don't mind her. She's just a little over-protective of me."

"Just a little." Jodie held two fingers up to indicate an inch.

"Well, I'm not doing her if that's what *you* think!" He smiled.

Jodie blushed. "I didn't say that. But apparently, you're thinking it."

He winked at Francie as she approached the table with the beers. "Thanks, sweetie!" A devilish grin spread across his face as his eyes met Jodie's.

"No problem. You want the usual tonight?"

His gaze remained on Jodie. "You see anything on there that looks good, or do you trust me to recommend something?"

She glanced at the menu. "I don't know about trust," she said jokingly. "But... I'll have what you're having, all the same." She handed Francie her menu.

"Okay, we want two of Snyder's all the works burgers with curly fries, please."

"Hold the pickles?" Francie asked.

"On mine. How about you, Jodie girl?

"Pickles are fine."

"Okay. Just give me a holler when you need another brew." Francie ripped off the order, slipped it into her apron pocket, and darted toward another table.

"See it's all fun and innocent!" Carlos smiled.

Jodie laughed.

She glanced toward two Hispanic guys entering and heading toward the bar. They seemed out of place compared to the others sitting at the bar. They were dressed in white tanks, homeboy jeans, and new Nike tennis shoes. They'd shaved their heads except for a strip down the center. Flashy Tattoos covered their arms and their jeans were so low Jodie could see the cracks of their butts when they climbed upon the bar stools. Tiny silver spoons dangled off silver chains around their necks, which was a symbol they were either coke users or drug dealers. She imagined that they were probably tied into a gang of some sort. She suddenly thought of the graffiti that had been painted across her door. A rush of nausea rippled through her stomach "Can you read graffiti?"

"What?"

"The letter K, what does that stand for?"

"Usually it means kill. Why?"

Jodie could feel the blood draining from her face. She quickly folded her arms across her stomach. "That's what I thought it meant."

"I didn't take you for the gang type, Jodie girl. Are you thinking about joining one?"

"No, never. How about you?"

"I've been tempted a few times, but work keeps me off the streets most of the time. I seldom get a day off."

65

Jodie was glad to hear Carlos wasn't involved in a gang. She'd been worried about the party he planned to take her to.

They drunk a few more beers after dinner and flirted continuously with each other. By the time they left the joint, Jodie was giggly and light-headed. Although it was easy to keep the conversation flowing, her mind occasionally drifted back to Nicole and the danger she could be in.

After several blocks, they rounded the corner at Bell Avenue, and Jodie immediately spotted a group of rowdy teenagers parading through a yard and into a single house dwelling. She had no doubt it was the party. She could hear the music pounding, distant chattering, and laughing. The neighborhood was run down, but nothing like the one she lived in. The houses were small and cramped together, but a few of them had nice yards. There were a few kids hanging at the corner, smoking cigarettes and trying to act cool. They couldn't have been older than thirteen. Jodie imagined they were already involved in a gang.

She followed Carlos into the house.

"You probably won't know many of these people because most of them are out of school or have dropped out," Carlos said.

"Okay. I probably wouldn't know them if they did attend our school. I don't socialize too often."

Carlos slapped a few guys on the back as he led Jodie through the house to the kitchen. "The good stuff is kept in here."

It only took Jodie a few seconds to realize he was referring to a huge keg sitting in the center of the room.

He reached for a couple of cups, filled them up, and handed one to Jodie. "Sorry about the foam." He guzzled his down and refilled his cup. "Come on—let's go outside where the action is."

She followed Carlos out the back door. "Whose house is this?" Her eyes were immediately drawn toward the hip-hoppers on the patio. There were six of them performing incredible stunts. She'd never witness such talented dancers before.

"Reece, he works with me as a dishwasher. He rents this place out with three other guys. He moved here from Phoenix.

66

He's hoping to be discovered as a dancer." He pointed toward a slim white guy, walking on his elbows. "That's him there."

"Wow, he's really good."

"Yeah, he's a cool dude and a hard worker. I hope he makes it one day." He pointed toward a Hispanic guy. "That's Fredrick." He continued to point out the others. "Jon, Simon, Adam, and Blake. They're all dancers. Jon and Simon have an apartment on the other side of Front Street, and Fredrick, Adam, and Blake live here with Reece." He nodded toward Fredrick. "I think him and Adam are an item, but I'm not sure."

"I'll never remember all their names," Jodie said.

"That's okay—they all answer to dude."

A tall, attractive blond in a black leather mini skirt and silver silk blouse rushed toward them. "Hi Carlos. You got a night off?"

"Yeah, finally—much needed too! Carli, this is Jodie."

"Is this your first time here?" She asked Jodie.

"Yes, I'm afraid I don't know anyone."

"Come on, I'll show you where the restroom is—guys never think of that." She rolled her eyes toward Carlos. "I'll bring her back shortly—that is if we don't get side tracked!

"Here, let me refill your cup while you're gone." He reached for Jodie's cup. "Do you need one, Carli?"

"No thanks, I'm a vodka gal." She pulled Jodie toward the house. "I live up the street, so I hang here a lot. I used to hook up with Jon, but we're just pals now." She led Jodie up the aged stairs to the restroom. "There's one downstairs, but it's always occupied." She knocked on the door, waited a few seconds, and turned the knob. "See, it's empty. Do you actually need to go pee, or do you just want to do a line?"

"I'll go while I'm here, but no coke for me. Thanks, though." Jodie slipped inside the small restroom consisting of a stained toilet, cluttered sink, and a dripping shower. She wasn't surprised that Carli did cocaine—every other person in New York did drugs now days.

Carli was still standing outside the door when Jodie came out. "Thanks for waiting."

"You're welcome. How about a valium?" She pulled her out grown bangs behind her ears as she reached in her pocket and pulled out a small-capped bottle. She popped the cap off and dumped some pills in her hand.

"No thanks."

Carli shrugged and swallowed a pill. "Well, if you change your mind, I'll be around. You know Carlos gets high with me sometimes."

"No, I didn't know. This is the first time I've been out with him."

She grabbed the rail on the stairs for support as she led Jodie down. "Well, he's a swell guy and he's not bad in the sack either, if you know what I mean?"

"What?" Jodie couldn't believe she was having this conversation.

She flicked Jodie on the arm. "Just kidding!" She threw her head back and laughed. "Don't worry, I haven't had your man, but he is good for the eyes. I bet he'd be smooth in bed! Let me know, okay." She winked.

Jodie told Carli she'd see her later and made her way back through the crowd. She spotted Carlos within a circle of guys. He introduced her to his friends, and before long, she was comfortably mingling by herself, while he helped carry in another keg.

She hadn't been drunk for a long time, but Carlos kept filling her cup, and before long, her mind grew numb. She didn't care that she was getting louder and sillier because it seemed like everyone else was too. She didn't mind at all when Carlos pulled her onto the patio to dance, or when he scooted up close to her and ran his hand over her rear. She didn't protest at all when he slid his tongue in her mouth. She was so caught up in the music and the pressure of Carlos's body up close to hers—nothing else seemed to matter. She didn't even resist when he led her up the stairs and into one of the bedrooms.

It wasn't until the next day when she woke that she'd realized what had happened. A thin sheet covered her naked body as Carlos slept soundly next to her. An unfamiliar black cat purred at her feet. She vaguely remembered coming to the bedroom. She remembered laughing at Carlos when he'd stumbled over a footstool, but everything else was a blur. She didn't remember shedding her clothes and having sex with Carlos. But she was sure it had happened.

She jumped up and collected her clothes scattered across the floor. She felt cheap and dirty. It wasn't the first time she'd had sex, but it was the worse she'd ever felt about it. She had really liked Carlos, but now he'd think of her as just another piece of meat.

She threw on her clothes, keeping her eyes glued to Carlos. She hoped he didn't wake up before she could sneak out. Maybe, he was too drunk last night and wouldn't remember anything. *Fat chance!* Guys never forget having sex, no matter how drunk they are.

She silently slipped through the bedroom door and crept down the stairs, stepping over a pair of high-heels and other articles of clothing. She covered her eyes as she passed a naked guy and girl asleep on the couch, peeking only long enough to notice the muddled living room. The stench of stale beer was so thick she thought she was going to puke. She tried to swallow, but her throat was too dry. She quietly made her way into the kitchen, which was even worse than the living room. Puddles of beer covered the floor and counters, and her shoes kept sticking to the floor. There weren't any clean glasses, so she stuck her mouth under the faucet and gulped down the cool water.

She hurriedly made her way back through the house and out the front door. The sun was shining brightly, which was like a hammer to her head. She squinted as she tried to remember the direction they'd come. She hadn't a clue what time of the day it was. But as she strolled down the block, the aroma of bacon and eggs confirmed that it was still morning.

She suddenly remembered Nicole and sadness overwhelmed her. Something was terribly wrong—she could feel it. She broke into a jog, and before long, sweat was dripping off her forehead. She quickened her pace. *What was it?* It wasn't the hangover or the sex anymore. Something was going to happen! Something *bad* was going to happen! She had to warn Nicole before it was too late.

Chapter Eight

By ten, Tara had already taken a shower, dressed, and ate breakfast. She'd been up since eight. She imagined her mother and father were turning in their graves about now. They usually couldn't get Tara up before noon on Saturdays. She assumed the early rising was due from going to bed so early—ten-thirty on a Friday night. She'd tried contacting a few old friends to see if any of them wanted to come and stay the weekend, but everyone was busy. She should have known better. She was too far from them now. Their lives had gone on without her. And she was stuck in the miserable apartment.

Tommy had to work later than usual, so she'd watched some documentary on serial killers. After watching awhile, she'd realized the show might effect her sleeping, so she'd flipped off the TV and went to bed.

Now she was refreshed and ready for anything that didn't involve sitting in the apartment.

She carried her cereal bowl over to the sink and then roamed toward the window. The street was already buzzing. Some older boys had already started a game of kick ball. Another woman was sweeping the steps of Jodie's building. Three elderly black men stood on the corner laughing and exchanging stories of some sort. A car honked at the boys playing ball, and a grumpy man leaned out the window and yelled for them to get out of the way.

71

Two young teenaged girls came be-bopping out of a building dressed in mini skirts, sleeveless tanks, and black high heels. They'd piled their hair loosely on top of their heads and wore more make-up than needed. They giggled and took off in the direction of the main strip. A middle-aged lady with swollen, blood-shot eyes pushed a stroller with a wailing baby up the street, while another lady that looked more like a man walked a spotted Dalmatian.

Tara's eyes watered as loneliness set in. Everyone had something to do or somewhere to go. Everyone except her!

Her eyes drifted toward a figure running down the street. As the individual neared, Tara opened the window and popped her head out. *Jodie? Surely it wasn't.* But it was her, wearing a wrinkled short sleeve top with huge perspirations spots. Her hair was ratty and sweat beads covered her forehead. "Hey, Jodie, what's wrong?" Tara shouted.

Jodie didn't blink. She bounded up the stairs and into her own building.

Tara slammed the window shut and locked it. She grabbed her purse and keys off the table and hurried out the door. She'd never seen Jodie so shaken. Something had to be terribly wrong. She prayed it didn't have anything to do with Snake.

She hurried across the street and into the building. She rapped hard on Jodie's door, not carrying if her mother answered. She was too concerned about Jodie.

Suddenly the door flew open, and Jodie stood, legs straddled, with the pistol aimed at Tara.

Tara gasped.

Jodie immediately dropped the gun to her side. "I'm sorry. I thought you were him."

"What? Who?" Tara asked, flabbergasted!

"Come inside." She grabbed Tara's arm and yanked her inside. "We have to hurry before my mom wakes up."

"What's going on?"

"I'll explain on the way." She dumped her mother's purse on the counter, snatched a couple of twenty's, and scooped up the rest of the change. "I'll answer to the wicked witch later. Let's go!" She slipped the pistol into her jacket.

Tara followed Jodie out the door and down the hallway.

Maddie poked her head out of her apartment door. "What's going on, Jodanne? What's all the chaos?"

"I don't have time to explain, Maddie. Nicole's in trouble, and I need to help her. I'll come by later if I can."

"Child, you worry me to death. Be careful and let me know something," she called out.

Jodie and Tara ran through the lobby and out the door.

Jodie quickly explained to Tara the painting on the door as she jogged up the street.

"Why didn't you go yesterday?" Tara didn't understand why she'd wait a whole day if she were so worried about her sister.

"I don't know. I could have taken the subway yesterday, I guess." She slammed her fist into the palm of her opposite hand. "*Why* didn't *I* go yesterday? Now if I'm too late, I'll never forgive myself."

"Where were you coming from earlier?"

Jodie rolled her eyes. "No comment."

"Carlos? You stayed with him, didn't you?"

"Maybe. I don't want to talk about it right now."

"Sure." Tara had no doubt that was where she'd been all night. She was surprised she'd stayed with him after only one date. She cursed silently at herself. Who was she to judge? She'd probably do the same thing if she could get a date! "Where are we going anyway?"

"It's too early for Randy, and I know a taxi would cost a fortune, so we'll have to settle for the subway."

Tara glanced nervously over her shoulder to make sure they weren't being followed. "I'm sure Nicole's okay."

"I hope so." She stopped to catch her breath. "You don't have to come if you don't want to."

"I'm not letting you take off on the subway by yourself. Besides, Tommy will be gone most of the day anyway."

73

After a few blocks, Jodie flagged a taxi down and instructed him to take them to the subway station. By noon, they were on the subway and headed for Queens.

"Are you going to tell me anything about your date last night?" Tara asked.

Jodie sighed. "Okay, if you must know, it was fun. We had dinner at his uncle's place and then we went to a party."

Silence.

"And?" Tara asked.

"What else do you want to know?"

"Well, you didn't come home until this morning. So, what happened? Did you stay all night with him?"

"We got drunk and crashed at the party."

"Did you sleep with him?"

Three elderly ladies dressed in purple suits and red hats suddenly ceased their chatter and glared at Tara and Jodie.

Tara lowered her voice. "Well, did you?"

"Are you writing a book?" Jodie rolled her eyes.

"No. I'm just really nosey." She grinned.

"Yeah, I did, but I don't remember it."

"Omigod! You had sex and don't remember it?" Tara covered her mouth with her hand.

One of the ladies in the red hats handed Jodie a card. "It's my church group. You're welcome anytime."

Jodie handed the card back to the lady. "No thanks." She whispered to Tara. "It's no big deal!"

"Well, it would be to me!"

The ladies remained quiet as they strained to hear the conversation.

"Can we talk about this later? We're creating a scene."

"Sure, but I want all the details."

They rode in silence the rest of the way.

Tara didn't think Queens was as near as intimidating in the daylight. She could still spot the prostitutes, though. They dressed in heels, revealing blouses, and flashy make-up. They mostly hung on the corners of the Boulevards.

74

The taxi dropped them off near the street they'd last seen Nicole. Although the lights on the bars weren't flashing, and drunks weren't stumbling out the doors, you could still tell it was a party area. And the streets were still full of people, probably getting an early start on the wild night ahead of them.

"I don't know if she'll be out yet. If not, I may have to try to find out where she stays." Jodie lit a cigarette and glanced up and down the street. She exhaled the smoke. "Right there." She nodded toward a girl on the corner. "I've seen Nicole with her before." She nudged Tara. "Come on."

Tara followed Jodie across the street.

"Excuse me." She tapped the lean black girl on the shoulder. "I don't remember your name, but I've seen you with my sister, Nicole."

"Oh yeah, I remember you." She chomped nosily on her gum. "I'm Celeste."

"Do you know where I could find Nicole?" Jodie asked.

Celeste blew a bubble, letting it pop loudly. "It seems like everyone is looking for her. She didn't come back to the pad last night. J.J.'s upset, too!"

"You're kidding! Are you sure? When was the last time you saw her?"

"Right before we went to work we grabbed a bite to eat at Maggie's Bar and Grill." Celeste pointed across the street toward a joint on the corner. "I haven't seen her since." She shrugged her shoulders. "If she was planning on running, she sure had me fooled." She glanced nervously up and down the street. "Hey, I better not be seen talking to you. J.J. might think I know something about Nicole's whereabouts, and I don't need him breathing down my neck." She rolled her eyes.

"I don't give a shit. My sister is missing, and I have to find her…"

Tara quickly interrupted, "I'm sorry for her outburst…she's just upset. Maybe you could give us her address, and we could keep an eye out for her."

Celeste's eyebrows furrowed. She hesitated as if she was debating whether to give the information out. After a few seconds, she replied, "Okay, it's 15145 Cornell Boulevard, Apartment 22, but *you* didn't hear it from me." She glanced again up the street. "I do hope she's okay." She blew another bubble. "There's so many fucking perverts any more." She waved to an approaching car. "Hey, I got to go now."

Jodie pantomimed pulling her own hair. "Sorry, but I'm really starting to lose it!" She paused. "I'm just really worried about her. Is there anywhere else she hangs out at?"

"No, this is her area." Celeste gestured up and down the street. "Good luck." She pranced over toward the car that had pulled up to the curb and stuck her head through the window.

Jodie bowed her head and cursed under her breath. "I can't believe this is happening, and it's all my fault!"

"Your fault? More like—my fault. I am the one you rescued from Snake in the first place."

Jodie shook her head. "If something happens to her, I'll never forgive myself."

"This isn't your fault. Come on, let's go find her." Tara headed west but suddenly stopped. "I have no clue where we're going."

"I'll run in here and get directions. Wait here." She ran inside the bar before Tara could respond.

After a few minutes, she returned. "Its a couple blocks over." She ran ahead of Tara, darting out in front of a van and causing it to screech on its brakes." The driver leaned out the window, cursing and waving the bird.

"You're fucking crazy, too!" Jodie shouted. She shrugged the man off and motioned Tara to hurry. "New York drivers are idiots! They act like they own the road."

Tara remained silent. She'd witness the incident and knew Jodie was at fault, but she wasn't going to say a word. Jodie was in no mood to tangle with. If there was any trait that Tara had learned about Jodie, it was that she was never wrong about anything—even when she was wrong.

Fifteen minutes later, they were beating on Nicole's apartment door.

A young, petite Asia girl with long, wet black hair, wearing a short terry-cloth robe answered the door. "Yes?"

"I'm looking for Nicole. Where is she?" Jodie was already pushing her way through the door.

"Wait. Who are you?" The girl stepped back, scared and confused.

Tara smiled at the girl. "It's okay. We won't harm you." She nodded toward Jodie who was already making her way through the house. "That's Nicole's sister, Jodie, and I'm Tara."

The girl was at Jodie's heels. "You need to leave before J.J. gets here," she said in a shaky eastern accent. "He'll be mad and then I'll be in trouble."

Jodie suddenly spun around and glared at the girl. "Where the hell is she?"

The girl took a step backwards. "She didn't come home last night." She glanced nervously toward the door. "J.J.'s out looking for her now." She paused. "You really should be leaving."

"Who was she with last night?"

"I'm not sure," she stuttered. "Only J.J. knows the clients."

Jodie continued through the apartment. She stopped at the bedroom. "Which bed is hers?"

The girl nodded toward the one against the wall.

Jodie darted toward the bed, yanked up the mattress, and snatched a diary. "Bingo! I know my sister too well." She slid the diary into her jacket. "Come on." She gestured to Tara and headed toward the front of the apartment.

Tara suddenly grasped Jodie's shoulder as her eyes traveled to the door. Standing in the doorway was the most callous looking black guy she'd ever seen. He had to be at least 6 foot five, and his chest was almost as wide as the door. He had long dreadlocks, a wiry moustache, and a neatly groomed goatee. His skin appeared as coarse as sandpaper, as though he might have had an acne problem when he was younger. A shimmering gold chain dangled from his neck and several gold-linked bracelets looped around one wrist, while an expensive looking gold watch circled the other one. A jagged faded scar across his cheek left no question about his character. And those dark eyes—*they could see right through her.*

Her heart raced as she nearly crumbled to the floor. She couldn't understand how she kept getting herself in these predicaments. She quickly said a silent prayer, although she didn't think God would be able to save her this time.

Chapter Nine

Jodie started to reach for her pistol but suddenly changed her mind. She dropped her hands back to her side and glared at the disgusting creep. She knew who he was—J.J. Saughter, one of the most feared pimps in New York City—word on the street was that he wouldn't hesitate to waste you if you crossed him.

Although there was nothing more she'd like to do than fire a bullet through his crotch, she at least had enough sense to realize that wouldn't aid in finding her sister. And that was her priority now. No matter how shitty nice she had to be to the low life!

Now that she stood directly in front of him, she wasn't near as frightened as she thought she would be. Although his looks were intimidating, she feared more for her sister's life than she did her own.

She remembered Maddie once saying; 'you don't know the power of your own strength until someone hurts your loved one.' *Was she referring to—killing the guy who shot her son?*

Jodie didn't blink as she waited for J.J. to speak.

His eyes slowly traveled up and down Tara and then Jodie. "What is your business here?"

Jodie knew the bastard let his eyes linger on her chest on purpose. "I'm looking for my sister Nicole."

J.J.'s eyes narrowed, his nostrils flared, and the lines around the corners of his mouth tightened. His left hand doubled up into a fist, and for a brief second, Jodie wondered if he was going to strike her.

"Well then, you must already know she's not here." He calmly took a step toward the Asian girl, who had shrunk back against the kitchen table. Suddenly, he grabbed the girl by the hair and jerked her head up toward the ceiling as Jodie and Tara gasped. "She hasn't made contact with you since I've been gone, has she, Lilly?"

"No, J.J.," she said in small, quivering voice. "I swear I don't know anything."

He let go of Lilly's hair and shoved her to the side. He took a step toward Jodie. "See, we got a problem. I'm looking for your sister, too." He rubbed his hand under his chin as though he was thinking. "You see, she has created a real dilemma for me."

Jodie pretended to scratch her stomach so her hand was near the gun. She could hear Tara's raspy breathing next to her. "Maybe I can help find her. Please, I think she's in trouble."

He leaned forward so he was within inches from Jodie's face. "And how do I know this isn't a set-up, and Nicole hasn't split?"

Jodie didn't budge, although the foul odor of his breath was retching. "Why would I come here today if I knew where she was?"

"To make me think otherwise!"

"That would be awful risky, wouldn't it? And if I *was* covering for Nicole, she'd never let me come here!"

He seemed to weigh her answer as he toyed with retrieving a cigar from a case. He lit the cigar, inhaled, and blew the smoke in Jodie's face. "All I know is that she has clients this evening and she better fucking show up soon…or maybe you'd prefer to take her place."

Tara quickly spoke up, although her voice was barely over a whisper. "My uncle is waiting outside for us. We really need to get going." She tugged on Jodie's elbow. "Come on, Jodie."

J.J. quickly stepped in front of the doorway and leaned casually against the frame. "Not so fast, ladies. I want you to make a note of this…" He paused as he exhaled smoke. "When I find Nicole, I'm going to teach her a lesson that she won't ever forget." His eyes locked with Jodie's. "And I will find her!"

80

Over my dead body, Jodie thought. Without thinking, she jerked the pistol out of her jacket and aimed it toward him. "I don't know where the hell my sister is—but so help me, I'll kill you if you hurt her."

Before Jodie could react, he grabbed her wrist and twisted it so the gun was aimed toward the ceiling. With his free hand, he easily wrestled the gun out of her hand. "I don't take kindly to threats." He aimed the gun at her head and squinted one eye.

Tara screamed while the Asia girl ducked behind the table. "Please, let us go," Tara pleaded. "Jodie's upset because she thinks a gang member is involved in Nicole's disappearance."

Jodie remained silent, too scared to move, and now her only weapon was in his possession.

"Jodie, is it?" he snarled. "Let me tell you something, bitch, you ever set fucking foot back in my building again, you better be prepared to go to work for me! Do you understand me?

Jodie reluctantly nodded.

"And," he continued, "if your sister doesn't show up soon, someone's going to pay for all the money I'm losing. If a gang has done something with her, I will find them and they will pay, but…" He squatted so he was looking directly into Jodie's eyes. "If it's someone else that is hiding her…they will pay. Are we clear?"

Jodie nodded again.

J.J. extended the butt of the pistol back to Jodie. "If you ever fucking aim a gun at me again I'll cut you up in so many pieces the authorities won't be able to identify you! Now, get the hell out of here."

Jodie, surprised, snatched the pistol and quickly slipped it inside her jacket. She grabbed Tara's hand and rushed through the door. Her heart was thumping violently against her ribcage. She ran toward the exit sign at the end of the hall. No way in hell was she waiting for the elevator. She quickly hurried through the door and down the stairs, skipping every other stair until she reached the bottom. She could hear Tara right behind her. They darted out the entrance door and sprinted down the block. Finally, at the corner, Jodie doubled over. "Ohmigod," she said, gasping for breath. "I really thought he was going to shoot me—with my own bullet!"

Tara didn't hold back the sobs. "Me too! I was so scared!"

Jodie straightened. Her breathing slowly returned to normal. "That was smart thinking, saying your uncle was waiting for us. He probably would have killed us, or even worse, made us go to work for him." She moaned—her side throbbed from running so fast. She rested one hand on her hip, massaging the sore area.

After a few minutes, they walked in the direction where they'd met Celeste. "I'm sorry. That wasn't very smart of me to go there. And I shouldn't have dragged you along with me."

Tara's sniveling ceased. "Are you kidding me? I know he would have shot you if you were alone."

"Well, maybe I deserve it."

Tara wrapped her arm around Jodie's shoulders. "Hey, quit it. I don't want to hear you talk like that. We'll find your sister." She led Jodie to a bench to sit.

Jodie suddenly broke. She'd held it back for so long—she couldn't stop the tears. All her life she and Nicole had to watch out for each other. They didn't have loving, caring parents like other kids. All they ever had was each other. If someone picked a fight with either of them at school, they'd always defend each other. If Jodie struggled with a subject at school, Nicole would tutor her until she understood better. If Nicole needed money for food or cigarettes, Jodie found a way to get it for her. It was just how life was for them. As long as Jodie had Nicole, she didn't care how their mother treated them. She could live without her mother, but she couldn't live without Nicole.

But something had gone wrong last year. Nicole couldn't take the every-day pressure from their mother any longer. Although she'd promised Jodie she'd return some day, Jodie had been skeptical. She wanted to believe that Nicole would come home, but deep down, she'd known it wasn't going to happen. And now, she might not ever see her again.

Tara spoke softly as she rubbed Jodie's back. "Don't give up. It's still early. Let's go ask around some more."

82

Jodie stood. "I'm not giving up." She cleared her throat. "Let's go. We'll spend the rest of the day looking for her here, and if we still don't have any luck, then there's just one thing left to do."

"Go to the police?" Tara asked.

"No... find Snake!"

***

Jodie wiped at the rain droplets dripping from her forehead and increased her speed. Only a few people that she passed had umbrellas, which meant she wasn't the only one surprised by the sudden rain. She jogged the last block and then hurriedly ducked through the entrance of Chester's.

She held her arms out and shook—water scattered from her like a wet dog. She'd left Tara's place with the intention of going home but changed her mind and decided to come to the pool hall to let Randy know she wouldn't be going with him. A storm had suddenly brewed up and within minutes, it was pouring.

She glanced outside toward the dark clouds. It was only a little after six, but by the looks of it, you'd think it was nine. The wind was blowing the sign over the pool hall, making it swing like a pendulum in a clock. Some people were holding newspapers over their heads. Others dashed into nearby buildings, while others continued at their normal pace, pretending the rain didn't affect them. She glanced toward the front of the bar where a group of men had gathered to watch the weather on the big screen TV.

She'd spent the whole afternoon in Queens, searching for Nicole but had come up empty handed. She didn't know anything more than she did before she went. And now all she wanted was a strong drink and many of them. She'd never been so frustrated.

Tara had tried to convince her to report Nicole's missing to the police. But Jodie knew it would never fly. Not only would the cops frown when they figured out Nicole was a prostitute, but if Jodie suggested Snake was responsible, then the gun issue

83

might surface, too. And more than likely they wouldn't even try to find Nicole. Prostitutes, pimps, thugs, and gang leaders were on the bottom of their list. New York cops had their hands full with drive-by shootings, rapes, and murders. They wouldn't have time to mess with a missing prostitute.

Jodie sighed and strolled over toward the bar. "Jack, I need a strong screwdriver, please."

"Bad day?" he asked with raised eyebrows.

"You could say that."

He finished mixing the drink and set it in front of her. "Well, maybe a few games of pool will cheer you up." He nodded toward the back of the bar. "Your friends are back there."

"Thanks." Jodie paid him and headed toward the back. She was sure Jack knew she wasn't 21, but ever since she flashed her I.D. over a year ago, he'd never questioned her. Of course, she continued to tip him good.

She caught a glimpse of Matt's red afro as she made her way back to the pool tables. Randy and Bronze were playing a game of pool.

Randy glanced up from his shot. "Hey, Flip, I heard you've been looking for me. You need a ride tonight?"

"I did, but I've already been." She sucked half her drink down in one swallow. "Nicole's missing."

"What?" Randy had been leaning over the pool table, but he suddenly straightened.

"Big sis?" Matt asked.

"Yeah, no one has seen her since last night." Jodie tried to keep the quiver out of her voice. The last thing she wanted was for these guys to see her break.

"That's not cool!" Bronze added.

"Where do you think she went?" Randy asked.

"I wish I knew." Jodie knew the guys were being sincere—Nicole had hung out with them several times before she found her other life. "I went to her apartment today, and J.J. Saughter showed up."

"What were you thinking?" Randy shook his head.

Matt agreed. "Yeah, he's bad news!"

Jodie rolled her eyes. "Yeah, big mistake! For a brief second, I thought he was going to kill me. Anyway, I'm not allowed back in his building again, which suits me fine." Jodie finished her drink and hollered toward the front of the building. "Start me another one, Jack."

"I'm on it," he yelled back.

"Hey, count me in." Bronze laid his pool stick down and wiped his hands on his jeans. "I'll go with you and help look for her."

"Yeah, me too!" Matt said.

"Thanks guys, but it's useless," she said flatly. She spun away from her friends and made her way back to the bar.

She was digging her money out of her pocket when a familiar tan arm reached in front of her and placed a twenty on the counter. "I've got it."

She instantly recognized the voice. She slowly turned around to face Carlos. She stood there speechless, staring up at him. It was as though her tongue was nailed to the roof of her mouth, and she was certain the blood had drained from her face.

Carlos snatched the change off the counter that Jack had laid down. "You're supposed to say thanks for the drink." He grinned.

"I'm sorry," Jodie stuttered. "Thanks."

"You want me to leave now?"

"No…I mean, not if you don't want to." Jodie moved toward the corner of the room, out of earshot from the others.

"I just want to know why you ran off this morning without waking me?"

Jodie stared down at the green faded carpet. "I'm sorry." She paused. "I guess I was embarrassed."

"Embarrassed? About what?"

"You know."

Carlos lifted her chin. "Did you not enjoy last night? Because I know, I did. Although I was drunker than hell, I won't forget last night!" He lowered his voice, "It was good between us. And I enjoy being around you."

85

Jodie looked away. "This is not a good time for me." She took a sip of her drink. "I sort of have a crisis going on?"

"You're just saying that because you don't like me, right?"

"No, really." Her eyes met his. "My sister is missing. I spent the day in Queens trying to find her." She brought the glass to her lips again, swallowing a larger amount. She was eager for the alcohol to kick in and numb the pain.

"Oh, wow." He rubbed her shoulder. "Let me help."

Jodie's eyes watered. "I don't think you can." Suddenly she had an idea. "Unless you can find out some information for me, about a gang in the vicinity."

He grabbed her hand and led her to a table. "Okay, fill me in. What do you know?"

She quickly explained to Carlos the situation, leaving out a few of the minor details. She told him she needed to know more about Snake's gang, but she didn't tell him why she needed to know, nor did he ask.

"There's a guy that I work with, Austin, he used to belong to a gang," Carlos said. "Somehow he managed to get out of it without being killed. Anyway, I'll see if he can help me out."

"Thanks." She downed the rest of her drink, relinquishing the lightheaded feeling. Tonight, she'd drown her sorrows, and tomorrow, she'd plot her revenge.

Chapter Ten

Tara made a peanut butter and jelly sandwich, and grabbed the potato chips off the counter. She poured a glass of coke and set it on the table. She shifted the chair so it was directly in front of the window, so she could watch the activity outside.

Tommy was working a double shift, so it would be late before he got home. It would be another boring evening.

As scared as she was of J.J., she was still glad she'd gone with Jodie. Not only for moral support, but also, for something to do. She was so sick of sitting in the apartment. Everyday it seemed like the walls were enclosing more in on her. She wasn't used to being closed up all the time.

She glanced out the window at the crowded buildings and narrow street. She thought of her old house and the big back yard. She missed the landscape view consisting of a rock garden filled with flowers of every color. Her mother had been the most creative gardener. Tara had spent many evenings doing her homework out on the patio. Her father would come home from work and start the barbeque grill and then pull up a chair to go over Tara's homework. If she had a history test the following day, he'd drill her with history dates until she had them all memorized. No wonder she'd always made good grades. She'd always had loving parents who encouraged her to be her best. A tear slid down her cheek and then another. She'd give anything to be back on her patio with her parents. If only she hadn't gone to the mall that particular Saturday. She grabbed a tissue off the table and blew her nose.

A crying baby from a stroller interrupted Tara's thoughts. The mother had stopped pushing the stroller to talk on a cell phone. The mother tried to pacify the baby with a bottle as she continued her conversation. The baby pushed the bottle away and increased his wailing.

Suddenly Tara's gaze lingered on the group of boys walking pass the stroller. A familiar red headband caught her attention. She gasped as she spotted the snake tattoo slithering out from under the headband as he turned to talk to his friend. She jumped to her feet as she tried to figure out which direction he'd come from. Had he come from across the street? Surely she'd seen him if he'd come out of Jodie's building.

There were five of them. Her heart was pounding fiercely. All of sudden Snake spun around and looked up toward her window. Tara hit the floor, but she wasn't sure if it was fast enough for Snake to miss. She gripped the legs of the chair and held her breath. The memory of that horrible night came flashing back. Finally, she slowly pulled herself to her knees and peeked over the edge of the windowsill. The boys were at the end of the block. She waited until they were completely out of view and then stood. She grabbed her keys and darted out the door. She didn't think they'd been in Jodie's building, but she needed to warn Jodie that they'd been snooping around.

She ran all the way to Jodie's apartment but hesitated at the door. The thought of Jodie's mother answering the door terrified her. She doubled up her fist, knocked, and waited. No answer. She repeated knocking several times but still no response. She could have sworn Jodie had said she was going home.

Maybe she'd stopped at Maddie's. She spun, jogged down the hall, and knocked on her door. Maddie peeped through the peephole and opened the door. The scent of fresh baked cookies filled Tara's nostrils.

"Come in, come in." Maddie reached for Tara's hand and pulled her inside. "You must have smelled them from the hallway."

88

"Actually, I didn't, but they do smell wonderful." Tara scanned the kitchen. "Jodie's not here?"

Maddie pulled a chair out for Tara to sit. "I haven't seen her today." She frowned. "Is anything wrong?"

"Oh no. I was just looking for her." Tara wasn't sure how much Maddie knew.

Maddie smiled and reached for a plate. She scooped up the cookies from the cookie sheet and set them on the table. "Would you like milk or juice?"

"Juice is fine. Thanks." Tara took a bite of the chocolate chip cookie. "Wow, this is good."

"I'm glad you like them. They were Jerome's favorite." She hung the potholders on the hook and pulled up a chair next to Tara. "Tell me, child, how are things going for you these days?"

"Oh, it could be better, but I guess it could be worse too?"

Maddie patted Tara's hand. "You poor thing. I know losing your parents must have been devastating. And then having to move to this neighborhood on top of everything you're going through. I know the schools around here are nothing to brag about either."

"It's definitely been a change. I do a lot of praying." She reached for another cookie. "Do you believe in God, Maddie?"

"Of course I do, child. I'd never of survived Jerome's death without God. There were days when I didn't want to get out of bed. I used to pray for God to let me die, but he had other plans for me, I suppose."

"Yeah, like Jodie. You're all she really has. She'd be lost without you."

"Yes, the girl worries me to death. And that mother of hers, I'd like to give her an earful."

"Do you think Jodie believes in God?"

"Umm, I don't know, come to think of it. I don't think it's ever been brought up. I just assumed she did."

"Sometimes she makes comments to make me think she doesn't."

"Have you asked her?" Maddie stood and retrieved the juice out of the refrigerator. She refilled Tara's glass.

"No, she can be so defensive sometimes."

"Well, child, maybe that is God's plan for you and me to help her see otherwise."

"I use to go to church camp every summer and retreats during the year. I don't know when I'll get to go again, but if I do, I'll invite Jodie."

"I think that sounds like a great idea."

"Do you believe our loved ones are with us after they die?"

"I used to wonder about Jerome a lot. I just prayed he made it to heaven." Maddie's eyes clouded over. "I've got to believe he did." She rolled her eyes toward the ceiling. "I believe that when we are in pain, they are with us in spirit."

"Sometimes I feel all alone, and I wonder if my mom and dad are anywhere near?"

Maddie patted her own heart. "They're right here always. Don't ever forget that. They'll always live within your heart, and you should never feel alone."

"Maddie, you're such wonderful person." She stood and kissed Maddie on the cheek. "I need to get back home before it gets late."

"Yes, of course. Saturday night, the worst night to be out after dark." She bagged up some cookies for Tara and walked her to the door. "You come back any time. I enjoyed visiting with you. You're going to do fine. Give yourself time to grieve." She hugged Tara.

"Thanks, Maddie."

Tara hurried back to her apartment. She quickly locked the door and leaned against it. Seeing Snake had brought back unpleasant memories, and she was actually glad to be back in the safety of the cramped apartment. She was sure the locks her uncle had installed were secure enough now. Although she realized if Snake wanted to get in bad enough, he could probably find a way. She glanced toward the window, although they were on the bottom floor, the window was still eight feet from the ground, which made her feel a little safer. But she'd still feel a lot better if Tommy was there. She settled in the chair in front of the window. The streetlights flickered on as the commotion outside slowly ceased. She knew it was going to be a long evening because there was no way she was going to be able to relax until Tommy got home. *And where was Jodie, anyway?*

***

It was after ten before Jodie got back to the apartment. She settled back in the faded brown armchair, flipped the TV on, and dug the diary out of her jacket. She was relieved her mother wasn't home from the bars yet. Although her mind was blurred from the alcohol, she couldn't wait until morning to read the diary.

She opened to the first page—it was back when Nicole still lived at home. She'd written about a history test that had been too hard, and about Derek, a senior that she'd had a crush on. Jodie flipped a few more pages and read about the cake that Nicole had burnt. Jodie giggled aloud. She remembered that day like it was yesterday. They were so worried that the burnt smell would still be lingering in the house when their mother got home. They opened the windows and burned candles, trying to get rid of the awful stench. Their mother was so toasted when she got home, she didn't even notice. She even ate a piece of the burnt cake and didn't even complain. All evening, every time Nicole would look at Jodie, they'd burst out laughing. They were still snickering when they climbed into bed.

Jodie brushed a tear off her cheek and flipped through the pages until she reached April. The writings from the first few days of April brought more tears to her eyes. Nicole wrote about some of her clients and some of the strange requests they had.

Suddenly, Jodie stopped and flipped the page back to the previous page. It was dated April 9 and the next page was dated April 17. Although Nicole sometimes skipped a day or two, it was unlikely that she'd skip that many days in a row. After a close examination, Jodie noticed the seams were uneven and pages had been torn out.

The more recent pages, April 22 and 23rd, were about J.J. and how much she admired him and respected him for taking her in

91

when she had no where else to go. "What?" Jodie said aloud. She couldn't believe Nicole would speak so highly of the scumbag. *Was she out of her mind?*

Jodie flipped through the rest of the pages, but they were all blank, which meant she didn't write yesterday, the 24th, the day she disappeared. She flipped back to March and skimmed through those pages, but still nothing out of the ordinary that would help her find Nicole. "Damn it!" She flipped the TV off and went to her room. She didn't want to be up when her mother got home.

Jodie tucked Nicole's diary underneath her mattress next to the pistol. She changed into her gown and climbed into bed.

She briefly thought of Carlos and how concerned he'd been tonight. He'd even walked her home. Her friends at Chester's had treated him like he was a friend of theirs. They had all played pool, and Jodie tried to be as cheerful as she could, but Carlos had sensed she was unhappy. He didn't even try to persuade her to stay out later when she'd told him she wanted to go home.

He'd kissed her goodnight, but it wasn't a wild passionate kiss liked they'd shared the night before. It was a gentle, caring kiss, and Jodie appreciated Carlo's empathy.

Jodie's thoughts flipped to Nicole, and a muscle spasm shot through her stomach like sudden cramps right before a period. She'd never been so scared in her life. She was certain something bad had happened to Nicole, and she wouldn't rest until she figured it out. She was almost positive that Snake had something to do with it. She wished she'd thought to take a picture of the graffiti on the door. In case she needed it later for evidence of some sort. But she'd been too worried about her mother coming home and finding it.

Jodie figured the drinks would help her sleep, but the longer she lay awake, the more sober she became. It was late when she heard her mother come in, and the bathroom door slam. She listened as her mother went into her room and shut the door. She waited until she was sure her mother was asleep and then she tiptoed into the living room to double check the lock on the door. Her mother was often known to forget.

She climbed back in bed and stared up at the oval shadow that had formed on the ceiling. She knew life wasn't supposed to be fair. And some were dealt worse hands than others. But sometimes she felt like she'd been born with a black cloud over her head.

She couldn't stop the tears from sliding off the side of her face and hitting the pillow. She didn't think she could live if she knew she could never see Nicole again. Small sobs escaped from the back of her throat. She didn't know anything about the God that Tara was always talking about. But if he did exist, Jodie was certain he didn't like her or her sister.

She believed pity was nothing but a self-destructive act. She usually despised people that felt sorry for themselves. But at that moment, she was drowning in fear, loneliness, and *mostly* pity.

Jodie's sniffling slowly ceased and then the turning and tossing set in. It was late into the night before she drifted off to sleep.

***

Tara had tried watching TV, but when the news came on, she'd gotten bored and ventured to the window again. There were still some traffic, and a couple groups of teenagers were hanging out on the corners at the end of the block. But none of them resembled Snake or his gang.

She'd been glued to the window most of the night except during three sitcoms. She was glad, too, or she would have missed Jodie being walked home by Carlos. She'd felt somewhat guilty watching them kiss goodnight. She wondered if Jodie had planned all along to meet with Carlos, or if it was a spur of the moment thing. Tara didn't think Jodie would purposely lie to her. But then again, Jodie liked to keep her personal life to herself. It was like pulling teeth, trying to get Jodie to fill in the details about her date last night.

93

Tara thought of her old friends. They confided everything in each other. She knew who they'd first kissed, who they secretly liked, and how far they'd gone with guys they'd gone out with. Tara knew when they'd started their periods and all their bras sizes. They'd even made up secret code words for when they passed notes in case it got in the wrong hands.

But Jodie was different. She wasn't anything like her old friends. She was quiet and more reserved. She didn't like to share her feelings. Tara had never heard her talk of any other friends, other than the guys at Chester's. She was starting to wonder if she even had any. All she'd ever talked about was Nicole.

The screeching tires of an older black Oldsmobile directly below her window interrupted her thoughts. Three guys in black ski masks jumped out of the car. *What the hell?* Before she could react, the guys pulled guns from behind their backs and aimed them directly toward her. "Omigod!" She screamed as she tried to duck out of the window's view. The shooting was sudden. Glass shattered and pieces flew everywhere. Tara fell to the floor, but not before she felt something hit her leg. Horrified, she tried to crawl away from the window, but the pain shot down the side of her leg. But her fear outweighed the pain, and she forced her weight on to her good leg and pulled herself away from the window. She tucked her chin to her chest and cradled her head with her arms—the way she was taught to do during tornado drills. She couldn't believe this was happening. She heard sirens in the distance. The shooting ceased as sudden as it started. She heard the squeal of the car pulling off.

She lifted her head. The sirens were growing closer. She tried to stand but it hurt too badly. She gasped as she looked down at the pool of blood her leg had created. "Ohmigod, I've been shot." She screamed louder than she'd ever screamed in her life. She kept screaming until her ears filled up, and she couldn't hear the sirens. Her head was spinning in every direction. Suddenly, the room went black.

Chapter Eleven

Jodie plopped down on Tommy's couch. "Wow, I can't believe this happened to you. I must have slept right through the noise."

"I'm glad it was just glass in my leg and not a bullet." Tara lifted her wrapped up leg onto the footstool.

Jodie watched the man as he finished replacing the glass in the window. He picked up his tools, accepted a check from Tommy, and shook hands. Tommy walked the man outside. She glanced back at Tara. "Tell me again exactly what you saw?"

"Jodie, I've told you everything up until I blacked out. I'm getting tired of repeating the story to everyone." Tara sighed and threw her head back against the headrest. "I'm sorry. I don't mean to be so snappy, but someone tried to kill me last night."

"I know. I just want to make sure it was Snake."

"Of course it was Snake. Who else would it be?"

"First, my sister disappears and now this. I can't believe he's going this far to get revenge." Jodie suddenly stood, strolled toward the window, and looked out. "Why were you watching out the window? Did you see me come home?"

"I was bored. And yeah, I saw you making out with Carlos."

"He just kissed me good night."

"Well, I saw it."

"The cops just pulled up. They are talking with your uncle." Jodie pulled up the kitchen chair and sat down near the window.

"Damn, they won't leave us alone."

"You're sure you didn't mention Snake's name?"

"I seriously thought about it, but I knew you wouldn't approve. I don't get it, either. Why don't we just tell the police what is going on? They can bust Snake, and we can forget about him."

"Because it would be our word against his, and there's no way to prove he's guilty and then he will kill us for sure."

Tara walked toward the window. "Well, I hate to break the news to you, but I think he's going to kill us, regardless."

Jodie's eyes hardened as she stared out the window. "Not if we kill him first."

Tara laughed. "Yeah, sure."

Jodie remained silent. She couldn't let Snake live if he'd done something to her sister. She thought of the Sally Field movie, '*An Eye for an Eye.*'

"Jodie, please tell me you're joking?"

"Okay, I'm joking." She stared out the window. She should have expected Tara wouldn't understand. She didn't have any siblings, so she couldn't possibly comprehend how horrible her situation was. She'd thought being shot at was traumatic, but it didn't compare to what Jodie was going through. She stood. "What time is it? I need to meet Carlos at noon."

"It's a quarter till."

She moved toward the door. "I better go."

"Why are you meeting him so early?"

Jodie hesitated. "He's going to try to help me find Nicole."

"Oh, okay—if you got to go."

"I'll stop back by later."

"I might not be here. We're supposed to go apartment hunting."

"You are?"

"We won't be moving right away, but we're getting closer. My uncle goes to talk to the lawyer on Tuesday."

"Lucky you. Well, talk to you later."

As she hurried toward Chester's, her depression grew. She'd always known that Tara wasn't planning to stay in the neighborhood for very long, but she'd gotten used to her living across the street and sort of liked it. She'd never had a friend before except Taylor in Geography class and Maddie. It was sort of cool hanging out with someone her own age.

She was a little envious, too. Jodie would give anything if she could just pack her bags and move away from all the troubles in her life, but she knew that was never going to happen.

A horn blaring made her jump. She hadn't been paying attention and crossed right in front of a taxi. She leaped out of the way, and the driver shook his fist and yelled something in Spanish. "Yeah, yeah, yeah, whatever." Jodie shouted back. She rounded the corner and glanced behind her to make sure she wasn't being followed. She patted her jacket pocket, a habit she'd picked up since she'd gotten the pistol.

She was anxious to see if Carlos had any information on Snake's gang.

As she approached Chester's, she spotted him on the bench, smoking a cigarette. "What are you doing out here? I thought you didn't mind my red-neck joint any more."

He grinned. "One night a week is enough." He glanced at his watch. "And you're late."

"I can't be that late." She sat down next to him.

"Two minutes."

She whacked him on the arm. "You're fussing over two minutes."

"I have to break you in right." He leaned forward and brushed her lips with his.

"That's what you think." She enjoyed the flirting, but she didn't think it was an appropriate time to be having butterflies. "Did you find out anything?"

"A little." He glanced up and down the street and lowered his voice. "Snake is his gang name, which you already knew. His real name is Tyrone Williams. His gang is an inner city gang called The Serpents. It's a rather new gang, and their members are low in numbers right now. They are in the recruitment stage."

"Is he from around here anywhere?"

97

"I hear his turf is over near Drexel. He's known for making trouble wherever he goes, though." He grabbed her hand. "Now, tell me, Jodie girl, what are you going to do with the information I just gave you."

"Um…I'm not sure."

"There has to be a reason you wanted to know all of this."

"I think Snake knows where my sister is."

"It sounds like this character is no one to mess with. I don't want you going anywhere near him."

Jodie shot him an annoyed look. "What do you suggest then?"

"I don't know yet. I'll have to think about it. Maybe we should go back to Queens and check to see if she ever showed up."

Jodie hesitated. "I think it would be a wasted trip, but maybe you're right."

"Let's go now. We'll grab a bite to eat while we're over there. I have to be back to work by this evening."

"Are you sure you don't mind?" She stood.

"Didn't I tell you I was going to help you find your sister?"

"Oh Damn, I can't." She sat back down. "Thanks, I appreciate the offer, but I'm scrapped. I spent all my money last night."

"That's why I work, so I can help beautiful woman in need." He leaned forward and kissed her.

She pulled away from him. "Why are you doing this for me?"

He looked puzzled. "What do you mean?"

"I'm sorry, but I'm not used to someone doing something for me in return for nothing."

"Who says I don't want anything?" He grinned.

Jodie knew exactly what he was implying. "Oh, so you're going to make me owe you?"

"You can pay me back however you like." He leaned forward and passionately kissed her. "For now, that will do." He stood and pulled her to her feet. "Let's go."

Jodie enjoyed the warm fuzzies in the pit of her stomach. She didn't know if it was his stunning looks or his casual flirting that turned her on, or maybe it was a combination of both. Whichever, she was just glad he was still interested after their first wild date.

He grabbed her hand, squeezed it, and raised his other hand to hail a taxi.

***

Tara followed Tommy through a two-bedroom apartment in an amiable, peaceful neighborhood. The apartment complex was on the edge of the city in a middle-class neighborhood. She'd have to locate to a different school, which was fine by her.

She excused herself from Tommy and the real estate broker, and slipped down the hallway for one last look at the bedroom that would be hers. She loved the feel of the plush carpet underneath her shoes as she walked across the room. She longed to feel it under her bare feet. She quickly slipped out of her shoes and curled her toes. She'd forgotten how wonderful it felt as the carpet tickled the bottom of her feet.

The room wasn't quite as nice as her old bedroom, but it would be a drastic change to where she was sleeping now—on the couch. It was painted beige and the carpet was a mixture of beige and brown. The trim was all in white. There was nothing fancy about the room, but Tara knew it had potential. She opened up the closet; it was clean and roomy. She glanced around the bedroom, imagining how she'd arrange her furniture. She'd be thrilled to finally be able to get her things out of storage.

Tommy had told her that her parents had left her money for college and some money after she graduated college. Her parents had also left enough insurance money for them to live comfortably for a while.

Tara hobbled over to the window. Her leg was getting sore from standing, so she shifted her weight onto her good leg and leaned against the ledge. She stared out the window. The scenery was such a pleasant change. The kids were playing in a nearby park rather than in the streets. Women dressed in fashionable clothes gathered in a Shelter house, preparing a luncheon of some sort. The streets were wider and there was even a parking lot for the cars. One man had pulled his car up in the park and was washing his car off with a hose.

Tommy stepped into the room. "Well, what do you think? I see it didn't take you long to kick your shoes off."

"I couldn't resist." She threw up her hands. "I absolutely love it. Are you sure we can afford it?"

"We'll be able to soon. I'll know more when I talk to the lawyer this week. Hopefully, in the next couple of weeks we'll be able to move. "I'm sorry you'll have to switch schools again.

"Are you kidding? That's fine by me. I'll miss Jodie and Maddie, but I can always go back to visit." She looked down at her leg. "Or maybe not."

"Once I get you out of that neighborhood, I don't want you going back. You've had nothing but bad luck since you came."

Tara frowned. "I wonder what will happen to Jodie?"

"I know she's been a good friend, and she'll always be welcome wherever we decide to move." He put his arm around Tara's shoulder. "I'm so sorry about last night."

"It's not your fault."

"If I lived in a better neighborhood, this wouldn't have happened." He squeezed her shoulders. "You have been through more in the last few weeks than the ordinary person experiences in a lifetime." He lowered his voice, "I just wish I could take the pain away."

"I'm okay, Tommy." She sighed. "At first I missed them so bad I didn't want to get up in the mornings, but as time goes by it gets better." She hugged him. "Thanks for everything you've done for me."

"I haven't been able to do much."

"You took me in, and you didn't have to. You're all I got, you know? And you've always been more of a big brother to me than an uncle."

"And you're all I got left. I'm so glad you're parents thought to leave me as guardian." He grinned and ruffled her hair. "Who ever thought we'd be living together, though." He grabbed her elbow and guided her toward the door. "Come on, let's go see if Mrs. Barker will hold this place for us."

She slipped her shoes on, took one last glance around the room, and followed Tommy out into the hall.

As excited as Tara was, the thought of leaving Jodie saddened her. Since Tommy had to work so much overtime, she'd leaned a lot on Jodie. Being around Jodie had made her grieving easier, and she'd miss her terribly. She quickly caught a tear with the back of her hand before Tommy saw it. She moaned as her leg throbbed against the bandage. She glanced down at it, and suddenly the guys in the ski masks blurred her vision. As painful as it was to leave Jodie, she knew she had no choice.

***

Jodie and Carlos paced the streets of Queens most of the day without any luck. Toward evening they spotted Celeste in a tavern with a slender bearded man.

Her eyes widened as Jodie approached her. She glanced nervously toward the front door, "What are you doing here? You need to leave before J.J. finds you here."

"I need to know about my sister. Has she been found yet?"

"Nope. And J.J. knows about you and your friend, Randy. Is that him?" She nodded toward Carlos.

"No! What are you talking about?"

"He knows about Randy dealing on his turf. But worse, he knows about him bringing you here, and you guys trying to persuade Nicole to come with you.

"Randy didn't have anything to do with that!"

Carlos interrupted, "Are you saying that J.J. thinks Jodie has something to do with Nicole's disappearance?"

"That's right, and I'm going to be a dead woman if I'm caught talking to you." She nervously chomped on her bubble gum as she glanced again toward the front door. "You need to get out of here."

"Damn it," Jodie mumbled. "Okay, we're out of here," she said, flustered.

101

Carlos reached for Jodie's hand. "Don't worry. He'll have to go through me first."

As much as Jodie appreciated Carlos bravery, she knew he didn't have a chance in hell against J.J., but she didn't say so. "Thanks, Celeste," she called over her shoulder and followed Carlos out of the bar.

Suddenly fear filled her insides as all the pieces of the puzzle came together. She knew J.J. was capable of anything. He wouldn't think twice about killing them. *Killing* to him was as natural as *eating* was to her. *And how did he find out about Randy?*

Now, she not only feared for Nicole's life but for her own and Carlos, too. She glanced nervously up and down the street, believing at any moment he would pounce around a corner and shoot them.

Carlos must have sensed Jodie's uneasiness—he immediately flagged down a taxi. "Are you okay? You're as white as a ghost."

"I just want to get away from this place. Nicole's not here."

"It's okay." He gave the taxi driver directions and then slid his arm around Jodie's shoulders. "We're going back now."

Jodie's fear subsided as they drove away from Queens. She didn't think she'd be able to go back there again. She was certain she wasn't going to find Nicole there anyway.

As they approached Chester's, her concern for Nicole returned, and she no longer feared J.J.

It was close to seven, and Carlos insisted that Jodie eat something. She hadn't eaten anything all day. He led her to a nearby outdoor café.

"I thought you had to work tonight," she said.

He pulled his cell phone out and tossed it on the table. "I called earlier when you were in the restroom. They said they weren't busy, and I didn't need to come in if I didn't want to."

"Oh. Well, thanks for your help today."

"You're welcome."

She slumped down in the metal chair and sighed. "But, it's useless. We'll never find her."

"Surely, someone has got to know something."

Jodie's eyes narrowed. "Snake knows." She banged her fist on the table. "He's done something to my sister and then if that wasn't enough, he tried to shoot Tara last night. What's he going to do next?"

"You don't know that for sure." He moved his elbows off the table, so the waiter could set down their drinks."

She told the waiter she'd have a bowl of potato soup, and Carlos ordered the same, adding on a club sandwich. The thought of food didn't appeal to her, but she needed to eat to keep her strength up. "I know Snake is responsible!" she hissed. "I'll make him pay if he's harmed Nicole in any way."

"Now, Jodie girl, don't be going and trying to be a hero." He winked but his face remained serious. "I know you're upset, but you won't help your sister any if you're sitting in a cell locked up." He lowered his voice. "Give me a couple days to investigate further."

Jodie rested her chin on her fists. "What are you going to do?"

"I have a few friends that have been around the block. They know the ropes when it comes to gangs. Maybe they can give me some more insight into this gang of Snake's."

"They're all evil as hell!"

Carlos leaned back on the two back legs of his chair. "What does your mom think about all of this?"

Jodie rolled her eyes. "She doesn't know!"

"What?" He leaned forward, causing the chair to hit the ground with a thud. "You didn't tell her?"

She shrugged. "It wouldn't matter. She doesn't care anything about Nicole."

"I know you don't get along with her, but are you sure you're not being too harsh?"

"Believe me, I'm not. If Nicole and I disappeared off the face of the earth, she wouldn't care!"

"I'm sorry. I didn't realize it was that bad at home."

She remained quiet as the waiter set down their food. She waited until he'd left the table before she spoke, "It's okay. It's a fact of life that I've accepted." She blew on the spoonful of soup. "How about you and your family?"

"My grandma raised me. And I believe she's done a damn good job of it!! Look at me." He grinned and Jodie laughed. "Actually, under the circumstances, I think she did well."

"Oh?"

"My mother got pregnant when she was fifteen. She didn't know who the father was nor had any desire to raise me. I guess she wanted an abortion, but she'd waited too long to have it done. A few weeks after I was born, she just packed her bags and left me behind with my grandma and grandpa. My grandma suspected she was using drugs." He paused. "Well, my loving grandparents took me in, but my grandpa passed away when I was five, leaving my grandmother to raise me by herself."

"Wow. Do you ever hear from your mother?"

"I've seen her, maybe, a dozen times since she left. She moved up to New Jersey and would visit sometimes during the holidays. As I grew older, the visits became less frequent. Sometimes she'd bring her boyfriend, who always seemed to be wasted. My grandmother would get angry, and then her and my mother would end up arguing." He sipped his hot tea. "And I don't think she's ever felt remorse about leaving me. I'd just prefer she didn't come around at all."

"Your grandmother must be one special lady."

"Like no other. One day I hope I can make her life as comfortable as she helped make mine."

"What about your uncle?"

"He's my mother's brother but complete opposites. He's fifty and never married. He wrapped his life around his business. For some reason, I think he feels somewhat guilty for what my mother has done. He's always treated me good. I can't complain about my upbringing." He grasped both her hands and leaned forward. "I'm sorry for what you have been through, and I know how important it is that we find your sister."

Jodie's eyes misted. It was nice to see Carlos had a serious side. She was thankful she'd accepted that first date with him.

104

But he still hadn't convinced her enough to change her mind. She knew what she had to do. Nicole would do the same for her.

She wanted answers, and she couldn't wait a moment longer. Time was ticking away, and every hour that passed by without Nicole was one less hour of hope. She had to find Snake, and she'd do whatever she had to do to make him cooperate. Although she was terrified of him, *she was more scared to find out the truth about Nicole.*

Chapter Twelve

It was a little after nine when Tara heard the knock on the door. Her breath quickened as her heart raced. Tommy had just left to run to the grocery store to get more bandages. *Oh God, what if Snake has come back to finish the job.* She jumped up and hobbled toward the kitchen. She quickly pulled out the silverware drawer and grabbed the largest knife she could find. Fortunately, there was a good size butcher knife. She tightened her grip around the handle and crept toward the door.

"Tara, it's me. Are you in there," Jodie called out.

"Ohmigod!" Tara jerked the door opened and pulled her friend inside. "You scared the crap out of me! I thought you were them."

"Who?"

"Snake and his gang." She placed her hand over her heart and dropped down on the couch.

"I only wish they were around, so he could tell me what the hell he did to Nicole. I know he's responsible!"

"So, *no* luck today?"

"Nothing. She never returned to Queens. We ran into Celeste again, and she said J.J. thinks Randy and I have something to do with her missing."

"Randy?"

"Yeah, I guess from that night he took us over there. And he also found out that Randy was dealing drugs over in his territory."

"I figured that was what he was doing." She motioned Jodie to sit as she adjusted her leg more comfortably. "Where's Carlos?"

"I told him I needed to go home because I knew he wouldn't approve of my plan."

"What plan?"

"I'm going to find Snake tonight!"

"What? Are you out of your mind?"

"I have to find him and make him tell me where Nicole is." She hesitated and then added with a quivering tone, "If he has killed her... I need to know."

"Do you think he's going to tell you?"

"He's going to tell me something—I guarantee it!" She patted her jacket pocket where her gun was hid.

"Jodie, you can't go looking for him. He'll kill you. Besides its Sunday night; we have school tomorrow." She just didn't get Jodie's way of thinking.

"I'm not going to school. I'm going to find my sister." She stood, folding her arms across her chest.

"Please, don't go. Stay with me until Tommy gets home, and we'll see what he suggests."

"I can't wait."

"I can't go with you. I promised Tommy I wouldn't leave the house."

"I didn't expect you to. I'm going by Chester's and see if Randy might give me a ride over to Snake's turf. I just wanted to let you know in case I end up missing, too."

"Don't say that. You're scaring me! Can't you wait until daylight?"

"I imagine he sleeps during the day. Besides, I want to catch him off guard; he won't be expecting me tonight." She opened the door.

Tara limped toward the door after her. "Jodie, no, please don't go," she begged, although she knew it was useless to argue with her, especially if she'd already made up her mind.

"I'll come by tomorrow." She turned and was out the door before Tara could say anymore.

107

"Damn it!" Tara raced to the window and watched Jodie jog up the street. "What do I do," she mumbled aloud. She paced back and forth in front of the window for a few minutes. Her mind raced to the night Snake had tried to rape her. She recalled how brave Jodie had been. Jodie could have left her to defend for herself, but she chose not to. And if it weren't for that night, none of this would be happening. She couldn't just abandon Jodie when she needed her more than ever now. "Damn it, Jodie!" She quickly scribbled a note to Tommy, explaining she'd gone with Jodie. She hurriedly grabbed her jacket and the mace. "God, be with me," she mumbled as she went out the door.

***

Jodie glanced toward the star-full sky as she jogged toward Chester's. It was a clear, dark night only a sliver of the moon was visible beneath a cloud. The air was crisp but not unbearable. Her jacket was plenty warm. As she reached Monroe Street, the city noises increased. The familiar traffic with blaring horns and distant sirens vibrated in her head. She squeezed passed a group of sightseers who were gawking at the architecture of a vintage theater building.

The streets were still full of people. Many of them probably coming from dinner or heading toward the clubs. Most people thought New York was overcrowded, but Jodie had been there for so long, she couldn't imagine life any different. For some reason, she was more aware of the surrounding sights and sounds tonight than she usually was. Maybe it was because she knew it could possibly be her last night in the vicinity. She couldn't deny the fact that Snake would probably kill her *unless she killed him first.* She shivered. She'd never imagined herself killing someone, but her sister's life had never been at stake either.

She glanced toward a mother, father, and young daughter coming out of Vinnie's Pizza Pub. They were laughing about something the father had said. For a slight second, Jodie resented the girl and her happiness. She was dressed in a stylish sweater with a matching scarf and designer jeans. Her eyes briefly locked with Jodie's as she passed by, and the girl smiled.

What the hell was there to be so happy about? She had a sudden urge to smack the smile right off the girl's face. Jodie hated happy families. Life was so friggen unfair!

She suddenly felt guilty for her corrupted thinking. She used to swear she wouldn't become one of those persons that felt society owed them for their unfortunate lives. Jodie believed it was the ones that felt sorry for themselves that ended up on drugs or homeless. She knew she shouldn't complain about her life—there wasn't a day that went by that someone on the street didn't beg her for food or money. She had it better off than many in the city.

Life was what it was. And if this were the day she was to die, then so be it—it wouldn't be a loss for anyone anyway since Nicole couldn't be found. Her mother could care less, although Maddie and Tara would miss her. She suddenly thought of Carlos—cute, sexy Carlos. *What was she thinking? She couldn't die now and leave him!*

As she made her way to the back of Chester's, she decided she wasn't going to take a bullet without a fight. Snake had better give her some answers!

She was surprised to see Bronze and Matt sitting at a table rather than playing pool. "Hey guys, what's going on?"

They exchanged uneasy glances with each other as they waited for the other to speak. Finally, Bronze cleared his throat, "Hey Jodie, I'm afraid we have some bad news."

Jodie knew it had to be serious for Bronze to call her by her name rather than Flipper. "Well, what is it?"

Bronze bowed his head and suddenly Jodie's heart sank. "Where's Randy?"

Matt spoke up, "I'm sorry, Flipper. They found him dead in an alley in Queens."

"No, you're kidding me?"

"I wish we were," Bronze said.

Jodie rubbed her temples. "I don't believe this!"

"Rumor has it that it was J.J. Saughter."

109

"Son-of-a-bitch! This is my fault. He thought Randy and I were responsible for Nicole's disappearance."

"Oh, I'm sure there's more than that to the story." Matt gulped down the rest of the beer in his mug. "I know Randy was into other stuff."

"Yeah, he was dealing on J.J.'s turf, but J.J. wouldn't kill him only because of that. There are always random drug dealers in the area." She tried to stop the tears but was unsuccessful. "They killed him because of me! And Nicole is missing because of Snake. And I'm going to kill that bastard!" She hit her fist into the palm of her opposite hand.

Bronze slipped his arm around Jodie's shoulder. "Don't do anything stupid, Flip. We don't need anything happening to you, too."

"I'm going to find the loser right now and let him know I'm not taking his shit any more!" She spun on her heels.

"Hey, hey, slow down there, Flip. I'll give you a ride. You don't need to be taking off by yourself," Matt called after her.

"Shit, I'm gamed too. If someone tries to fuck you over, there're going to have to fuck me over first." Bronze downed his beer and slammed the mug on the table.

Jodie was hurrying through the front door when she nearly collided with Tara. "What are you doing here?"

"I'm not going to leave my best friend to defend herself. Not after all she's done for me," Tara said.

Jodie glanced down at Tara's leg. "What about your leg?"

"I'll manage! I made it down here, didn't I?"

"Well, more bad news," she paused as she tried to remain calm, "Randy's dead. J.J. did it."

"Oh my God! What is happening?" Tara's hand flew over her mouth.

"You don't need to go with me. Tommy will be furious with you." She called over her shoulder, "Matt, can you drop Tara off at her place first."

"Sure," Matt said.

"No way! I'm going with you guys. If you don't let me go with you, Jodie, I'm calling the police and telling them everything that's been going on!"

"You wouldn't?"

"Yes, I will."

Jodie hesitated. "Okay, but you're staying in the car because you won't be able to run."

"Okay, no problem."

Jodie didn't like the idea of Tara tagging along. Not only was she worried about Tara's safety, but also, it seemed like bad luck followed the girl. First her parents were killed and then she'd almost been raped, and now, she'd been shot at.

Jodie jumped into the front seat of Matt's Ford Focus, leaving the back seat for Bronze and Tara. "Shotgun," she called out. She quickly slammed the car door.

"Where," Tara screamed and ducked.

The trio laughed.

"You're too much," Jodie said.

"Don't do that. Remember, I just got shot at."

Laughter filled the car. Jodie enjoyed the humor for a change. She knew it wouldn't be long, though, and the atmosphere would drastically change.

***

Jodie pulled the gun from her jacket and laid it down on her lap as they neared Drexel. It was obvious that they were in gang vicinity a few blocks before they hit Drexel. Graffiti covered poles, road signs, and vintage buildings. Most shops had been abandoned, and boards covered their entrance. A few had iron bars across the windows and doors.

Jodie's adrenaline increased, and she wondered if everyone in the car was as nervous as she was. It was so quiet in the car she could hear Bronze puffing on his cigarette. A cigarette would definitely calm her nerves. She reached for her pack but suddenly changed her mind. She didn't need any kind of distractions.

111

She soaked in every inch of the neighborhood as Matt cruised slowly down the street. Jodie hadn't seen a soul. There weren't any moving vehicles in sight either. It was as if the area was completely deserted. They came to a four-way stop, and Jodie was about to have Matt swing down a different street but up ahead at the next intersection were five guys interacting with some kind of hacky sack. "Go that way." She nodded toward the group.

"Are you sure, Jodie?" Matt asked.

"Go for it!" Bronze said. "I got her covered." He held up a small pistol.

"Jodie, why don't we just go to the police?" Tara begged.

"Shhh." She waited until the car was a hundred feet or so from the group. She rolled her window down half way to view the gang. "He's not with them," she whispered.

The gang members all turned and were staring and waiting…they started walking toward the car. The brawny one in the red tank and matching red bandana shouted toward the car, "It looks like we have some lost souls in the wrong place at the wrong time." He gripped a heavy club. "What are you looking at, bitch?" He screamed as he neared Jodie's window.

Jodie quickly rolled the window up and shouted at Matt, "Go, go, go! Let's get out of here."

Matt didn't hesitate. He slammed his foot on the gas pedal and the car sped out. The gang continued to run after them. Jodie spun around and gripped the car's seat as she watched the gang chase after them. More gang members were joining the group from every direction. "Damn, where they all coming from?"

"Gangs usually post themselves on every corner and then they signal each other when someone comes into their territory," Bronze said.

A few blocks later, the gang was out of sight, and other traffic could be seen. Jodie spun back around and sighed. "That was close. How do you know so much about gangs, Bronze?"

"Hey, I wasn't always a redneck. I've been in a few fights in my days."

112

"You, in a gang? I'd never suspect." Jodie said.

"I didn't say I was involved in a gang. Let's just say I know how they operate."

Jodie glanced at Tara. She was slumped down in the seat. Her trembling hands folded it in her lap. "Are you okay, Tara?"

Tara dabbed at the few tears that had slid down her cheeks. "I think so. I was just really scared."

"No need to be scared when I'm right beside you." Bronze winked.

Tara nodded and turned to stare out the window.

Jodie laughed. "No offense, Bronze, but if that was supposed to cheer her up, I don't think it worked."

"Hey—hey guys, look. Isn't that two more of them? They must be on their way back to their turf," Matt said.

Although the guys were still two blocks away, Jodie knew by the way he walked that it was *him!* "It's him! Slow down." She rolled her window down, gripped the gun with her right hand, and leaned forward.

"Oh God, I think I'm going to throw up," Tara mumbled.

"Stop when you get closer to him," Jodie whispered to Matt.

"What ever you do, don't get out of the car." He glanced in the back at Bronze. "That goes for you, too."

"Don't worry, I won't as long as they don't give me any reason to." Bronze shifted forward on the seat.

"You don't have to worry about me," Tara said in a trembling soft voice. "I'm not getting out."

Matt and Bronze chuckled as the car came to a stop at the four-way stop.

Matt coasted slowly as Jodie positioned herself sideways on the seat. "Okay, get ready to pull over. Do it fast, so they don't have time to react. Don't anyone say anything! I don't want to screw this up!" She took a deep breath as the pistol shook in her hand. The sight of him made her even more furious.

Seconds later, Matt pulled to the curb and slammed on his brakes within a few feet from Snake and his partner. Jodie leaned out the window, aiming the gun toward Snake. "Stop you son-of-a-bitch, or I'm going to blow your fucking head off!"

113

Snake glanced toward Jodie and quickly reached for something behind his back. Jodie fired the pistol to the left side of him, and Snake quickly reacted by holding his hands up in the air, along with his partner. Tara had screamed when the shot was fired and Jodie could hear her sobbing loudly from the back seat. "I'm not playing around, you bastard. I want some answers and I want them now!"

"Ask bitch and then you better say your prayers," Snake hissed.

"I don't think I'm the one that needs to be praying right now!" She was so mad at all that he'd done to her and Tara. It took everything she had to keep from pulling the trigger again. "I want to know what the hell you did to my sister?"

"Who?" He glanced passed Jodie toward the back seat of the car. "Well, if I'm not mistaking the bitch is in the backseat."

Tara moaned.

"Don't play stupid with me. You know who I'm talking about! Where's Nicole?"

"Nicole who, bitch? What the hell you talking about? I don't know any Nicole!"

"You fucking liar! What did you do with her?"

"You know what, bitch? You're fucking crazy, and I'm tired of playing your punk-ass games." He brought his arms down to his side.

"I'll shoot!" Jodie gripped the pistol tighter.

"You'd better shoot me now, bitch, because if you don't I'm going to blow you away!" He reached behind his back and flipped out a shiny black gun.

Jodie, impulsively, fired her pistol, hitting Snake in the side of his thigh.

Snake clutched his left leg and dropped to his knees. Although his face cringed in pain, he still aimed his gun toward Jodie and squeezed the trigger. Jodie screamed and ducked just as the bullet shattered the glass from the side view mirror.

Matt floored the gas pedal and peeled away from the curb.

Snake's partner dove behind a bush and continued to shoot at the car.

114

Tara screamed hysterically in the backseat, while Bronze continued to shoot toward the bush.

Matt drove away from the scene, and Jodie thought she'd done had a heart attack. She placed her hand over her rapid beating heart. "What have I done?" Although she'd told herself, she'd shoot him if she had to. She really didn't think she would have to. She just assumed he'd cough up the information she needed. But he'd caught her off-guard, and once again, her impulsive behavior had caused all the chaos. "What have I done," she repeated as though she was the only one in the car. Now she had no doubt if he did have Nicole, he would definitely kill her. She glanced at Bronze in the backseat, trying to console the sobbing Tara. "I'm sorry, Tara. I'm so sorry!" She turned back around and stared out the passenger's window. "He's not ever going to let me forget this."

Chapter Thirteen

Tara had never been more relieved to return to Tommy's apartment. She didn't even mind the scolding Tommy gave her for going out. Although she reckoned she should tell Tommy about the earlier episode, she couldn't bring herself to do it. She knew it would cause even more alarm. He was so worried about her as it was.

She tried to keep her head bowed as she scurried into the restroom to take her bath, but her red splotchy face must have been a dead give away.

Tommy stopped her just outside the door. "You've been crying?"

"Umm… yeah I was earlier tonight when I was talking to Jodie about moving." She tried to sound sincere, although acting wasn't one of her best skills. "We both got a little teary-eyed."

"Oh, I know it will be hard at first to get used to another school and all, but believe me, you will be much better off. And you'll have your own room."

"I know. I'm not upset about moving away from this neighborhood or the school."

"Well, why the tears then?"

"It's going to be hard to leave Jodie. I know that's hard for you to understand, but girls are different in that kind of way."

"My offer still stands, she can visit any time. Maybe on the nights I work late, she can stay all night and keep you company."

"Thanks, Tommy. I'd like that."

He glanced toward her leg. "How's the leg?"

"It's doing a lot better."

"I want to see it in the morning before you go to school to make sure there's no infection."

"Sure. Thanks, Tommy." She stood on her tiptoes, kissed him on the cheek, and proceeded on into the bathroom.

She stared at the reflection in the mirror as she waited for her bath to fill. Her eyes were red and swollen, and traces of mascara were smudged underneath them. Her lips were chapped and raw from gnawing on them. Her face was as pale as the porcelain sink. Her hair was unsightly. She picked up the brush and attempted to run it through the mess. It was matted underneath and it took several minutes to get the tangles out. "What more could happen," she whispered to the mirror.

After all the horrible events Tara had witnessed, she'd hoped being shot at might be the end to all the drama. But now she knew it would never end.

Another tear slid down her cheek as she stepped into the hot water on one leg. She still couldn't believe Jodie shot Snake. She lowered herself into the steaming water, draping her bad leg over the side of the tub. She sighed with pleasure as the muscles in her body responded to the heat. If only she could just stay in the tub for the rest of her life. She leaned her head back and closed her eyes.

She thought of her mom and dad, and suddenly wished she were with them. Frustrating tears splattered into the water. She used to wish that they were still alive, but now she wondered if they were the ones that were better off. Life had gotten so complicated lately.

She remained in the tub for at least twenty minutes. By the time she came out of the restroom, Tommy had already gone to his room. She gathered her books and homework up, so that would be one less thing she had to do in the morning. She spread the bedding out on the couch. Tommy had pushed the couch up against the far wall of the room, completely out of view of the window, so at least she wouldn't have to worry about being shot at while she slept. She quickly glanced toward the front door as a

117

disturbing thought surfaced. *What's stopping Snake from busting the door down and shooting her?*

Tara quickly dropped to her knees and held her hands in a praying position. *Please, God, help me. I know I have many faults, and I really didn't mean it when I said I didn't want to be here any longer. Please watch me through the night and let me stay on this earth another day.*

Tara glanced back toward the door. It was going to be a long night because she knew she wouldn't be able to sleep a wink.

***

Jodie was wired. The drinks she'd had with Bronze and Matt hadn't fazed her. It was after midnight when she finally decided to go home. She still hadn't decided if she was going to school in the morning. She really didn't want to go out without her gun. It would probably be best if she skipped tomorrow. Besides, she didn't feel much like school. Her mind was still on Nicole, although she'd almost convinced herself that finding Nicole alive was slim.

She made a glass of tea and peaked into her mother's room. She was glad her mom wasn't home from the bars yet.

She'd just sighed with relief when the front door opened, and her mother stumbled through the door. "Oh shit, not tonight," Jodie mumbled under her breath. She pretended not to see her and proceeded toward her bedroom.

"Jodie," Sheila shouted. "Come here."

Jodie stopped in her tracks and weighed her options. If she ignored her, *all hell would break loose,* but if she acknowledged her, *all hell would break loose.* Damn, the bad luck. She spun around. "Yeah, what is it?"

"Dinner? Where's it at?" Sheila asked with a slurred voice. She tripped over the edge of the rug and grasped the back of the couch to keep from falling. "I'm starved." She made her way into the kitchen. "I told you to have dinner ready!" She flung open the fridge. "There's not a fucking thing in here."

118

Jodie remained silent. She'd learned from experience sometimes silence was better with her mom. She knew her mother had never asked her to cook dinner. It was just a reason for her to bitch about something.

"Why the hell can't you do anything around here?" She pulled out a bowl of molded ravioli and flung it toward the wall. The bowl shattered and the ravioli splattered everywhere. "Clean this shit up!" She reached into the cabinet above the sink and pulled out a bottle of alcohol. She twisted the cap off and guzzled a huge amount down. She glared at Jodie. "I said clean this shit up!" She clumsily pulled out a chair from the table and flopped down in it. "Cook me something to eat. I'm hungry."

Jodie stared at her mom. She hated her more than she hated anyone in the world. She used to feel sorry for her, but that stopped years ago. She couldn't pity someone that treated their own life as worthless. "Nicole's missing." She didn't know why she said it—she hadn't planned to say it.

"Speak up. What you talkin about?"

"I said Nicole is missing, and *she may be dead!*"

"Don't shout at me!" She rubbed her temples as if she had a headache. "Nicole's missing? Yeah, right, whatever. That girl's always looking for attention of some sort." She took another swig and wiped her mouth with her sleeve. "The whore's probably out screwing someone right now!"

"You're sick! How could you talk like that about your own daughter?"

"Because it's true, and you're going to end up just like her. I see the way you carry on when I have men over, shaking your ass and all!"

Jodie rolled her eyes. "Yeah, like I really want some of those losers you bring home!" Some days she just didn't know when to keep her mouth shut. "Why did you even have kids? It's obvious you don't know anything about raising them."

"You know what? You need to shut your fucking mouth before I shut it for you!"

Jodie saw the fire in her mother's eyes and knew she'd hit a raw nerve. She didn't even have time to duck before a glass hit

119

her in the side of the head. She clutched her head and ducked toward her room. Luckily, the glass didn't break until it hit the floor, or it probably would have cut her ear.

"You bitch, get back in here and cook something for me," Sheila shouted down the hall.

Jodie grabbed her jacked and her purse. She was glad the pistol was still in the pocket. She grabbed a blanket and ran toward the front door.

Her mother had made it to the kitchen doorway and was leaning awkwardly against the frame with a steak knife in her right hand. "Get in here, bitch, and peel some potatoes."

Jodie stopped at the front door, spun around, and glared at her mom. "Go to hell!" Her mother lunged toward her, holding the knife above her head. Jodie pulled the front door shut just as the knife hit the door. Jodie ran full speed toward the lobby door. She should have known better to sass her mother while she was holding a knife.

She stepped outside and shivered. She was glad she'd brought the extra blanket. It was going to be a long, cold night. Although the street was deserted, the shooting from earlier spooked her, and she ran the distance to her hide away spot.

She lit the candle until she had her cot made up and then she blew it out. She pulled the covers up to her chin, trying to shake off the chill. She rubbed her hand over the side of her head and cringed. A small goose egg had formed.

Jodie tried to shut her mind off from the earlier incidents, but she couldn't seem to do it. She stared out into the dark for what seemed like hours. Every time she closed her eyes, horrible visions of Nicole's mangled body would appear.

Finally, signs of daylight peeked through the boards, and Jodie relaxed some. She slowly drifted off to sleep. And this time, only visions of Snake appeared. In the dream, he had only one leg, but he could run as fast as someone with two legs, and he was chasing her all through the city. Jodie kept trying to hide, but he kept finding her and then he'd start chasing her again.

Jodie woke in a sweat and sat straight up. She glanced toward the boards over the window, half-expecting Snake to remove them at any second. After several minutes, she lay down and fell back to sleep. This time she didn't dream.

***

Jodie waited until she was sure her mom had left the apartment and then she snuck back home. She slept most the day, while waiting for Tara to get out of school. It was after four by the time she'd showered, dressed, and hurried down the hallway. Maddie must have been near her door because she called out as soon as Jodie passed.

Jodie spun around. "Hi, Maddie."

"Everything okay?" She frowned. "You haven't been by?"

"I'm sorry, Maddie. I've been trying to find Nicole?"

"What do you mean—you're trying to find Nicole?"

"I'm sorry. I just assumed you knew. Nicole's been missing for a few days, and no one seems to have seen her."

"Oh my." She opened her door wider. "Well, I hope she shows up soon." She motioned her to enter. "Come in, and I'll fix you something to eat."

Jodie hesitated. "I just ate—but thanks." She nodded toward the lobby door. "I really need to go. I'm on my way to Tara's."

"Sure. Although I miss you stopping by, I'm glad you have a friend. Tara's a nice girl."

"Yeah, she is. I'll try to stop by soon, I promise."

"Okay, be careful, child."

"I will." She tapped her jacket pocket to indicate she still had the pistol that she'd given her. She waved, jogged down the hall, and dashed outside.

She kept her hand near her pocket as she darted across the street. She knew Snake would retaliate; she just didn't know when. She'd have to keep her guard up at all times.

Tara peeped through the new peephole in the door and then pulled the door open. "Hi. You missed school," she said more as an accusation than a question.

121

"I didn't know you were taking role call." She didn't wait for Tara to ask her to sit. She pulled out a chair at the kitchen table. "When I got home last night my mom had other plans for me."

"I'm sorry. Did you have a bad evening with her—on top of everything else we went through?"

"You can say that. I had to sleep in my spot, and I didn't sleep much of the night."

"I know what you mean. I didn't sleep much either, *but I still went to school.*" Tara grinned. "I think I'm madder because I had to *run* to and from the bus stop by myself. I was scared shitless! I ran all the way home today."

"I'm sorry. You should have skipped."

"I couldn't. Tommy wouldn't have let me without an explanation, and I don't want him to know anything about last night."

"Well, grab your purse. Let's go unwind at Chester's." Jodie stood.

"Are you kidding? Don't you think Snake's going to be looking for us?"

"Maybe, but we can't hide out forever. Besides, I need a drink to get rid of the blues I'm feeling." She quickly rummaged through her purse. "Damn, I forgot I didn't have any money. You got any?"

"Zilch! My allowance stopped the day my parents were killed."

"Well, I'll figure out something. Come on."

"I don't know, Jodie. Tommy doesn't want me out."

"He won't know. We'll be back before he gets off work."

Tara sighed and snatched her purse off the table. "You're determined to get me killed, aren't you?"

"Well, not intentionally." Jodie laughed as she led the way to the door.

"Oh, Carlos asked about you today in school." Tara followed Jodie out of the building.

"He did?" That was another reason Jodie wanted to go to Chester's. She was hoping Carlos might show up.

"Yeah, and he looked like he wanted to say more, but he didn't."

"What do you mean?"

"He just started to say something else and then changed his mind." Tara glanced back over her shoulder.

"Umm." Jodie kept her hand on her pocket as her eyes darted up and down the street. "I guess you can't jog with your leg like that, can you?"

"If we're this scared while it's light out, what are we going to do tonight when it's dark out?" Tara jumped up and down and shrugged. "I think I'm okay to jog. It doesn't hurt as much today."

"And I'm not scared! I just feel like jogging." Jodie broke into a slow jog.

"Yeah, whatever." Tara giggled. "Did you just realized that it is harder for a bullet to hit you while you're running?"

Jodie rolled her eyes. "Just be quiet and try to keep up."

Tara laughed and jogged silently beside Jodie.

Once they hit the strip, Jodie slowed to a walk. She figured there were too many people around for Snake to try anything. Besides, it was still daylight. She hurried into Chester's, all the same.

Bronze was leaning over the bar, drinking a beer, and watching the big screen T.V. "Hey, Flip." He nodded toward Tara. "Hi Tara. What are you girls doing here so early?"

"I could ask you the same question, but I won't if you spot me for a drink?"

"After last night I think *you* should be buying *my* drinks." He grinned and hollered toward Jack. "Get these girls what ever they want tonight."

Tara quickly added, "I just want a coke."

Jodie wasn't sure if Jack would have carded her or not. "I'll take a coke, too, with some friendly Jack in it, Jack." She winked at him, spun around toward Tara, and whispered, "I'll share."

Tara snarled her nose. "I don't want any whiskey, and you shouldn't be drinking any either. You have school tomorrow."

"Now *you're* my mother." Jodie said, annoyed. She turned toward Bronze and popped him in the arm. "Thanks, man. I owe you." She glanced toward the empty pool tables. "You up for a game?"

"Maybe just one. I can't hang out too long today. I have things to do."

"Like what? Polish your bike?" Jodie grinned. "Sure, I understand."

She moved to the back of the bar and had just racked the balls when she spotted Carlos out of the corner of her eyes, making his way back to her.

He grabbed her shoulders and spun her, so she was facing him. "We need to talk." He glanced around the room. "Now!" He pulled her to an empty table.

Jodie couldn't imagine why he was so pissed. "What's wrong?"

He shoved her down in the chair and sat directly across from her. He leaned forward so he was just a few inches from her face. His forehead had beads of sweat across it and his dark eyes narrowed as he glared at her. "Please tell me it wasn't you?"

"What are you talking about?"

"Snake was shot last night, and word is that it was a girl from this area."

Jodie bowed her head. She focused on a crack in the table as she struggled for words.

After a few seconds of silence, Carlos hit the table with his fist. "Damn it, Jodie, what have you done?" He stood and paced a few steps and then sat back down. "You lied to me last night. I thought you were going home."

Jodie hesitated and then lifted her head. "I'm sorry, Carlos. I really am, but I knew you wouldn't approve." She tried to place her hand over his, but he pulled it away. "I didn't mean to shoot him. It just happened." She couldn't control the tears any longer. "I just want my sister back." She sniffled. "I wanted him to tell me the truth about Nicole, but he wouldn't.t." She didn't know how to make Carlos understand. "He went for his weapon and I

124

fired. I was scared." This was the most she'd confided to anyone in her whole life. "I'm so sorry I didn't tell you."

Carlos remained silent while staring deeply into her eyes. Jodie wished she could read his thoughts.

Finally, he covered her hands with his own. His tone softened, "Jodie, this is bad." He shook his head. "This is so bad." He cleared his throat. "I forgive you, but I'm afraid Snake and his gang won't. Word is they are going to make you pay." He glanced away momentarily. "I care about you that's why I'm so upset, you know?"

"Thanks Carlos, but what's done is done. I can't do anything about it. I know it was stupid of me, and now, I'll have to live in fear."

His voice wavered, "You know I'll do anything to protect you…" He squeezed her hands. "But to be perfectly honest with you, I don't know if I'll be able to save you from a whole gang."

Jodie's tears ceased. "It's okay. I don't expect you to. You've done more for me than anyone in my life has done, and it hasn't even been a week since our first date." She grinned. "Don't worry, I'll be okay. He's all talk. He won't do anything. Besides, I'm not scared of him." She guzzled the rest of her drink. So far that was the biggest lie she'd told yet. She knew if she even made it through the night alive it would be a miracle. And she learned very early in life that there were no such things as miracles.

Chapter Fourteen

Tara could tell Carlos was upset and seemed to be lecturing Jodie about something, but she couldn't hear what they were saying. Maybe she could if Bronze wasn't so darn distracting. He couldn't let her sit in silence. He had to keep asking questions about her leg and then the drive-by.

She was dying to know what was going on. Finally, her curiosity got the best of her. "I'll be back," she told Bronze. She made her way across the room. "Everything, okay?"

Jodie glanced from Carlos to Tara. "Just the obvious—Snake is pissed off!" She laughed. "I should have aimed higher!"

Tara's heart raced as her fear increased. "Let's go home, Jodie."

"That would probably be the smart thing to do," Carlos agreed. "We'll catch a taxi, and I'll ride with you two." He stood.

"I'm not going anywhere. I just got here!" She shouted across the room to Jack, "I'll take another one."

"Jodie, do you not realize how serious this is?" Tara asked, annoyed. Sometimes she wondered what went though that head of hers.

"Chill, my friend. We'll be okay," Jodie said.

"Tara's right, you know. It's not smart to be out after dark," Carlos said. "You need to take his threat serious and be cautious for awhile."

Bronze silently approached the table and pulled up a chair. "Talking about last night?"

"I'm not—they are." Jodie rolled her eyes. "You guys need to relax." She walked toward the bar.

Tara shook her head and lowered her voice, so Jodie couldn't hear. "Don't worry, she's really scared. She's just trying to cover it up. And I don't think she'll do anything stupid to jeopardize her life." She glanced toward Jodie as she returned to the table and added, "I hope anyway."

She remained quiet as Jodie played pool with the boys. Every few minutes, she'd glance toward the wall clock. She was worried about beating Tommy home. He'd be furious if he found out that she was out again.

Nearly an hour later, Jodie was nursing her third drink, and Tara was getting impatient. She was certain Jodie was feeling a buzz because she was acting all giddy and flirting with Carlos.

She couldn't believe Jodie was handling the situation as if it didn't exist. She usually stayed more focused—it was as if she was starting to give up a little. She hadn't even mentioned Nicole's name all night.

Finally, Carlos demanded that Jodie go home. "Come on, Jodie. I'm not taking *no* for an answer. Let's grab a taxi before it gets any later."

"Yeah, I need to get home before Tommy gets off," Tara said, relieved.

"Okay, okay. I can see when I'm not wanted."

Bronze glanced at his watch. "And I stayed way past what I intended." He glanced around the bar. "I wonder where Matt is." He shrugged. "After last night, he probably decided to stay home. He never did have much guts."

"Guts?" Tara blurted. "If that was about having guts, I don't have any either!"

Carlos shook hands with Bronze and led the girls outside.

Tara shivered and ran her hands up and down over her arms. She'd wished she wore her jacket, but it had been a lot warmer earlier. She searched through the crowd of people swarming the sidewalks, but she didn't see Snake or anyone that resembled his

127

gang. She stayed close behind Carlos as he flagged down a taxi. Her stomach was queasy—she was sure it was her nerves. She couldn't wait to get back to the apartment and off the streets.

She remained silent as they rode back to their neighborhood, while Jodie and Carlos chatted nonstop. As soon as they pulled up in front of the apartment Tara knew something was wrong. An ambulance was pulling away from the curb and a group of spectators stood watching. "Oh my God," she mumbled. All she could think about was Tommy. "I'll talk to you guys later. Thanks, Carlos, for taking us home." She dashed up the steps to her apartment. The lump in her throat wasn't dissolving. *What if Tommy had came home early, and Snake had broken into the apartment?* The tears quickly surfaced. What would become of her if something happened to him? *Please, God, don't let this happen to me again,* she prayed.

***

The sight of the ambulance quickly sobered Jodie up. She was worried about Maddie. Although there were many other elderly people living in the building, she couldn't shake the nagging sensation. "I need to check on someone. I'll see you later." She quickly brushed his cheek with her lips. "Thanks."

"Hold on." He grabbed her arm. "I'm staying with you until I know you're safe inside."

"You don't have to."

"I know, but I'm going to."

The crowd had scattered, and many had ventured into their own buildings. Jodie hurried up the stairs with Carlos at her heels. She immediately spotted Maddie standing near her apartment door and sighed with relief. She hadn't realized how much she loved that woman until that very moment. The last few years had been rough, and Maddie had been the one to make a difference in her life. She'd encouraged Jodie and comforted her through the most difficult times. She'd fed her when she was hungry, and doctored her physical and emotional wounds from her mother. She'd filled the shoes of a grandma that she'd never had.

By the time Jodie reached Maddie, she knew something wasn't right. She had that ghostly look in her eyes like she'd had the night her son was killed.

Maddie nervously glanced up and down the hallway. "Jodanne, get inside." She opened the door wider and then quickly changed her mind and pulled it shut as her eyes settled on Carlos. "Who is he?"

Jodie wasn't quite sure how to answer. "Umm, he's a good friend." Carlos cleared his throat, and she quickly changed her mind. "He's my boyfriend." She glanced toward Carlos and was relieved to see he was smiling.

Maddie's eyebrows furrowed. "I didn't know you had a boyfriend." Her eyes locked with Jodie's. "Okay, get inside." She opened the door and motioned them both inside. She quickly closed and locked the door. She pointed to the kitchen table. "In there." She waited until they were seated. "I'm afraid I have some disturbing news."

"It's Nicole?" Jodie wasn't ready. She'd been dreading this day. She was sure Maddie was going to tell her they'd found Nicole's body in the river or something. Her heart pounded fiercely and her eyes clouded over. She was unaware of Carlos reaching for her hand.

"It's not Nicole, child. It's your mother." She paused. "She was shot by a gang member, and the ambulance took her away to a hospital.

The wild pounding in Jodie's chest suddenly diminished. "What happened?" Her mind was numb—she still couldn't believe that it wasn't Nicole.

"I heard she was out front, returning home, and a car drove by, and someone with a face mask leaned out the window and shot her. They said the bullet hit her in the shoulder."

"I bet it was Snake's gang." Carlos rubbed the top of Jodie's hand.

"But Nicole's okay, right?" She searched Maddie's face for the truth.

129

"Have you heard a word I've said, child?" Maddie rested her hands on her hips. "Do you realize what this means?"

"I'm sorry, Maddie. I'm trying to feel compassion for my mom, but it's hard to do." She sighed. "Is she going to be okay?" She secretly hoped she was dead. She bit her tongue as if to punish herself for thinking such a thing.

"I don't think its life threatening, but I'm not sure. It's you that I'm concerned about. A young professional woman was asking questions about you and Nicole?"

"Why?" She glanced from Maddie to Carlos. "You think they want to know about Snake?"

"No. She was probably a social worker and looking for under-aged children," Carlos said.

"Well, that's stupid. I'm not going anywhere with her. I've been taking care of myself my whole life."

"I knew you would feel that way." Maddie crossed the room to the stove and returned to the table with a plate of cookies. "That's why I told her you weren't around any longer."

"You did?" Jodie reached for a cookie and passed one to Carlos. "You'll love these," she told him.

"I told her that you and Nicole had run off more than a year ago." She poured milk in two glasses and set them in front of Carlos and Jodie. "I wasn't quite sure what to do, but I know how foster homes scare you, so I reacted the way I thought you'd want me to. I told the lady your mother lived alone."

"You're the best, Maddie! Thanks."

"That doesn't mean the lady will take my word for it. She'll probably be back."

"She'll probably contact the school to confirm it, too," Carlos added.

"Well, I won't go to school until my mom comes home. I'll do whatever it takes to stay out of the system."

Maddie shook her head. "You need to go to school, girl." She paused. "And you need to be prepared if your mother doesn't make it." She paced in front of the sink. "You know you're welcome to stay here, but I don't know if the courts would allow it. They may think I'm too old and cranky." She grinned for the first time since Jodie had arrived.

Jodie stood and kissed her on the cheek. "Don't you worry about it, Maddie. I'll come up with something! I need to get going."

"You're not going to the hospital, are you? That woman may be there."

"No, I'm going to go report to Tara what's happening and then I'm going back to my apartment." She glanced toward Carlos. "I hope this was Snake's revenge, and he's got his retaliation out of his system."

"I hate to see you mixed up with this gang. They're nothing but bad news." Maddie turned toward the window and stared out.

Jodie was sure she was thinking about her son.

She turned back around. "I'll call the hospital after while and see how your mother is doing."

"It was nice meeting you." Carlos shook Maddie's hand.

She looked Carlos squarely in the eyes. "She's a special girl, you know? Can I depend on you to make sure nothing happens to her?"

"Yes you can, I promise."

Jodie was almost to the door when Maddie stopped her. "Wait a minute." She crossed the room to her purse and returned with a wad of bills in her hands. She crammed them in Jodie's palm. "You'll need money while your mom's gone."

"I'm not taking your money, Maddie. I know you don't have much." She tried to shove the money back into Maddie's hand.

"Yes you are, girl, and I don't want to hear another word about it." She pushed Jodie out into the hallway and shut the door.

Jodie shrugged. "There's no use arguing with her." She started to stick the bills into her purse but quickly changed her mind and crammed them into her jeans pocket. Although it was unlikely, she'd be mugged before she got home.

"Wow, this is horrible," Carlos walked Jodie across the street to Tara's. "I'm sorry about your mom."

"Well, don't be because I'm not."

131

Carlos frowned, and Jodie realized how callous she must have sounded. "I know that sounded cruel, but you have no clue what kind of woman she is."

"But she's still your mother."

He'd hit a nerve! She spun toward him. "I didn't expect you to understand." She stopped outside of Tara's door and glared at him. "You know I can find my own way home. I don't need your help."

Suddenly he had her pinned against the wall, his face within inches of hers. "God, you're hot when you're furious." He tried to kiss her, but she quickly turned her head. "Playing hard to get just makes me want you more." He kissed her neck. "Now I got to have you."

As much as Jodie tried to stay angry—the butterflies in her stomach increased and it was only a matter of seconds before she was giving in to his kisses.

He slipped his hand up under her shirt. "Oh Jodie, I want to be with you," he said as he caressed her breast. "I promise it will be different this time. I'm not drunk."

Jodie's nipples hardened as her thighs went numb. She wanted him just as much. If Tara's door hadn't flung opened, she wasn't sure how far they would have gone.

"Okay, guys, I can hear you inside my apartment."

Carlos quickly dropped his arms to his sides and wiped at his mouth. "Sorry."

Jodie grinned. She'd never guess Carlos to embarrass so easily. His face was crimson red, and he looked like a young boy that had been caught with his hand in the cookie jar.

Jodie quickly filled Tara in on all the details about her mother. She didn't want to waste any more time than necessary. She was eager to get back to her apartment to continue with Carlos where they had left off.

Of course, Tara was full of questions, so it took longer than Jodie had anticipated.

By the time they got back to Jodie's building, Maddie was coming out of her apartment. "Jodie, I was just coming up to your place. I called the hospital and had a heck of a time getting any information. I finally told them I was an aunt and got a little bit out of the nurse. She told me your mom was in the intensive care unit and was in stable condition." She paused. "I just thought you'd want to know. It will probably be days before she's released."

"Thanks, Maddie." Jodie was thrilled her mother wouldn't be home for a while. She couldn't believe she was going to have the apartment all to herself. She quickly excused herself from Maddie and hurried up the hall.

Jodie unlocked her apartment door and held the door open for Carlos. "Welcome to my castle."

"Any place of yours is a castle to me." His lips were all over hers before she could get the door shut. He suddenly pulled away. "Is this bad timing for you with everything going on?"

"Are you kidding? It's perfect timing." She quickly showed him the small apartment, saving her bedroom for last. "And this is my room."

He glanced around the room. "I couldn't help but notice your bed." He winked. "It looks really soft."

Jodie leaned forward and kissed him. "Just so you know I've never had anyone else in it before." She was starting to second-guess his intentions. She stared down at the floor. "I don't normally sleep around, you know?"

"Is this what you think this is?" He lifted her chin.

"I'm not sure."

He sat down on the bed and pulled her down next to him. "I know we haven't known each other for very long. But what I feel for you is real."

"But why me? You could have any girl in the school."

"Because you're different and you're not fake. You speak your mind, and I like that." With raised eyebrows, he added, "Besides, you look pretty damn good, too!"

Jodie grinned. "You know when I first saw you I thought you were a macho dude who would be arrogant. But I was pleasantly surprised. I didn't think hot looking guys were nice." She glanced away. "I've never met anyone like you before. I thought guys like you only existed in dreams." She cleared her throat,

133

trying her best not to be emotional. "I've never had anything good happen to me, and I'm scared." She looked up at him with tears in her eyes. "I'm really scared. Snake tried to get back at me by shooting my mother. What if…"

"He takes his revenge out on me?"

"Yes."

"That's not going to happen." He leaned back on the bed, pulling her next to him, so her head was resting on his chest. He gently massaged her hair. "Jodie, I know your life has been rough but not everything has to end badly. Life can be good, you know."

"Not for me."

"It can and it will, but you have to be more positive." He kissed the top of her head.

"I'm trying, I really am." She lifted her head and kissed him. "Thank you for being patient with me." She closed her eyes, savoring his body so close to hers.

The rest of the night was a blur. She didn't sleep much, and for once, she didn't mind either.

Chapter Fifteen

Tara found a seat at the front of the bus and sighed as she sat down. She was glad it was Thursday, and the last class was finally over. She'd made it almost through the whole week without any drama. Jodie had resumed classes on Tuesday, but for some reason, hadn't shown up today. She usually came by the apartment before school but not this morning. Tara prayed it wasn't because of her mother.

Jodie still hadn't gone to see her mom at the hospital, but Maddie had informed her last night that there had been some complications with her liver. Jodie hadn't seemed to care much, and after what Tara witnessed, she couldn't half blame her. Sheila wasn't a nice person when she was drinking.

Tara's main concern was Jodie, and what would become of her if something did happen to her mother. She feared she'd be thrown into a foster home, and Jodie wouldn't oblige easily.

Tara's mind wondered back to Sunday night when she'd caught Jodie and Carlos making out outside her door. Envy stabbed at her heart as she thought of Mick. It seemed like ages since she'd had a boyfriend. Sometimes she wished she had a guy to talk to about her problems. She'd loved to have someone to lean on when she'd been attacked, or when she'd been shot at. And she'd love to have a boyfriend walk her home from the bus stop every day. She wouldn't be so frightened all the time, and Uncle Tommy wouldn't be near as worried.

Jodie and Carlos had been together ever day this week. Jodie didn't come bang on her door all the time like she used to. Now Tara had to go hunt her down, and Carlos was always with her. Sometimes Tara felt like a third wheel, the way they pawed each other like they couldn't wait to be alone. She was certain they were having sex, although Jodie would never admit it.

She silently shrugged as she thought of her old friend, Lacy. If it were Lacy having sex, she'd call Tara in the middle of it to tell her about it. Tara smiled silently—Lacy had always confided her deepest secrets with her.

She quickly flicked a tear with the back of her hand and stared out the window.

A horn blaring broke her trance, and then another horn blared, and another—traffic jam. The city was too big! There were way too many people, too many streets, too many stores, and too many schools. She hated the city. She glanced from the mob of people on the sidewalks toward the sky—smoke drifted toward the clouds, which explained why she was always coughing.

After a while, the bus stopped and Tara stood. She hurriedly squeezed in the middle of the other students as they filed off. She didn't want to draw any unnecessary attention to herself in case Snake's gang was nearby. She kept her head bowed and followed the others up the block.

Usually around the second block, everyone started going their separate ways, and today was no exception. She was glad it was close to seventy degrees and more people were on the streets. She didn't start getting nervous until she turned off the strip. The last three blocks toward her neighborhood were side streets and not as many cars traveled through them. She immediately increased her pace to a fast walk. She usually waited until the end of the first block before she started running, otherwise she'd be too out of breath. Sometimes she'd run the first two blocks and walk the remaining block. She couldn't decide which was better, *until she saw him standing ten feet in front of her,* and then she knew she'd made the wrong decision. And now it was too late to run.

She froze in her tracks. She knew her luck had finally run out. Her mind went numb as she recalled that horrible night when he'd brought the knife up to her throat.

The queasiness in her stomach increased as she reached for the mace on the side of her purse. It wasn't there, and she suddenly remembered she had removed it prior to going to school.

She trembled and took a step backwards as he took a step forward. He was dressed all in black again, and he still wore the red headband. He didn't look much different from the last time she saw him except for the white bandage sticking out from the bottom of his shorts. She noticed he wasn't carrying a weapon but that didn't mean he didn't have a gun within reach. She glanced around but didn't see any other thugs, although they could be hiding nearby.

He cocked his head. "Yo, Tara Woodward. What's your hurry?"

Oh God, he knows my full name. There wasn't any way to go around him unless she ran into the street, but she knew he'd easily catch her. She could turn and run the opposite way, but she didn't think her legs would carry her. It was taking all her strength now not to crumble to the pavement.

She remained frozen and speechless.

"Where's your sister?"

"What," she stuttered. "I don't have..." she gasped for air. It was if her lungs suddenly couldn't function. She couldn't talk, let alone scream.

"Don't play dumb with me, bitch. You know I'm talking about Jodie James!" He took another step toward her and shook his finger at her. "You know, bitch, I don't even know Nicole, but if I find her, I won't hesitate to kill the slut. Your sister fucked up when she fucked with me!"

Tara's jaw dropped. *Oh, God.* It suddenly hit her. The message on Jodie's door wasn't meant for Nicole—*K Fucking Sister Bitch.* It was meant for her.

Her knees buckled and she almost collapsed. She knew for sure now, the drive-by wasn't at random like the police had suspected. And now he was going to kill her in daylight, right in the street.

She wanted to flee, but she couldn't move.

Snake snickered. "Is Jodie's mom dead, yet?"

"I don't know," She mumbled as she glanced across the street toward an elderly couple, hoping they would look her way. But even if they did, she was sure they wouldn't jeopardize their own lives to help her. Jodie had told her that most people look the other way when they witnessed crime in this neighborhood.

He rubbed his chin. "You know, there are too many bitches parading around on my turf!"

"Please, just leave me alone." She wiped at the fallen tears with the back of her hand.

"I can't do that! You see...you and her fucked up...!" He reached his hand inside his short's pocket.

Tara held her breath. She knew death was near.

The screeching of tires startled both of them.

Snake quickly dropped his arms back to his side, and Tara prayed like crazy.

A lime-green Honda Element came to a sudden stop, and a girl leaned her head out the passenger window, glancing from Snake to Tara. "You're Jodie's friend, aren't you?"

Thank you, God. Tara didn't recognize the girl, or the older gentleman driving but didn't care as long as they didn't pull away. "Yes, I am.

"I'm Taylor. I have a class with Jodie, and I've seen you with her before. I'm trying to find her apartment. She left her notebook with her assignments on her desk yesterday, and she didn't come to school today, so I thought I'd drop it off. I know she'll need it."

"I can take you there. I live right by her," Tara offered quickly. She kept her eyes on Snake as she took a side step toward the car.

He seemed hesitant as if he wasn't sure what to do.

"I'd appreciate it," Taylor said. "If you don't mind?"

"I don't mind at all." Tara edged her way toward the car door—never lifting her eyes from him.

138

He shuffled his feet against the sidewalk and reached inside his pocket.

She gasped, but he suddenly changed his mind, spun the other way, and jogged across the street in front of the car.

Tara quickly opened the car door and climbed in. She wanted to lie down in the seat just in case he decided to turn around and shoot them all, but she decided against it. In the two short blocks home, in between sobs, Tara rattled off all that had happened since her parents had died. She didn't care if Jodie got mad at her for telling—she couldn't live in fear like this any longer.

Taylor's father, Derek, pulled up in front of the apartment building and shifted the gears into park. "You have to go to the police, Tara. You can't let this punk get by with this. I would be glad to help you out?"

"I'll have to talk with Jodie. She's going to be mad now because I told you guys."

"It sounds like she doesn't have any faith in the police," Derek said.

"Dad, you got to help her," Taylor pleaded.

"I will—if Jodie's willing. Would you like me to talk to her now, Tara?"

"Probably not." She could imagine how hot Jodie was going to be. "I better talk to her first and then I'll get back with you."

He handed Tara a business card. "Call me, and I'll see what I can do."

Taylor handed Tara the notebook. "Here, you can give it to her. Tell her I hope to see her tomorrow and to call me if she wants."

"She doesn't have a phone, but she's welcome to use my uncle's phone. I just don't know if she'll want to get out, but I'll tell her." Tara opened the door. "Thanks so much for saving my life. I think he would of killed me right there."

"Be careful," Taylor called out.

"Hey, I pick up Taylor after school everyday; I'd be glad to give you and Jodie a ride home from school for awhile."

Tara was overwhelmed. "That is so nice of you. My uncle can't get off work. Won't it be out of your way though?"

139

"It's okay. I own my own business, so I don't have to report to work at any certain time." He rubbed Taylor's shoulder. "I don't like her to ride the bus either. She's going to a private school next year." He snickered. "These public schools are a joke. I feel sorry for you kids now days. Anyway, I'll be by the side door tomorrow after school if you need a ride."

"Thank you so much for all your help." She slammed the car door shut and ran the rest of the way to Jodie's apartment. She couldn't believe she'd escaped death once again.

***

"Tara, calm down. I can't understand you." Jodie had witnessed Tara hysterical before and imagined she was overreacting again.

"Do you want a glass of water?" Carlos asked.

"Yes, thanks." Tara sniffled.

Tara drank the water and then took a deep breath. She patted her eyes with a tissue, calmly placed her hands in her lap, and told Jodie and Carlos all that had happened since she'd gotten off the bus.

Jodie moaned, "Why did you have to tell Taylor and her father?"

Tara glared at her. "Did you hear me? He was going to kill me!"

"You can't blame her, Jodie," Carlos crossed the room and stared out the window. "That thug's bad news."

"Oh, and the message he left on your door was for me not Nicole."

Jodie straightened. "What do you mean?"

Tara told her exactly what Snake had said.

Jodie threw her hands up in the air. "So I did it for nothing! You mean it wasn't even him." She paced. "This is friggen great! And where is Nicole then?"

"Don't be too hard on yourself," Carlos said.

"And now I'm to blame for my mom being shot, and if she dies it will be my fault." As much as Jodie hated her mom, she sure didn't want her mom's death hanging over her head the rest of her life. And even worse, if her mother lived, she'd make Jodie's life miserable if she found out what she'd done. "I can't believe this is happening." She shook her head. "It's never going to end!"

Tara was sobbing again.

Carlos crossed the room, back to Jodie, and placed his hands on her shoulders. "Everything will work out."

"Yeah, when we're both dead," Tara added.

"Come on you two." He shoved Jodie down in the chair and massaged her shoulders as he spoke to Tara, "I don't think he would kill you in daylight with people around. He may be evil, but he's not stupid."

"You didn't see him or hear him," Tara said.

"He's just trying to scare you."

"And he's accomplishing that well!" she snapped.

The knock on the door silenced the room. Jodie's first thought was the social worker. Carlos had told her he'd been in the office yesterday when a social worker had come in and mentioned her name. She knew it was just a matter of time before they caught up with her. She'd been hoping to get through the last two weeks of school before they came searching for her, but it didn't look like she was going to make it. She tiptoed to the door. She was certain it wasn't the landlord because the place was paid up until the end of May.

 She waited.

"Jodie, its Maddie, open up."

Jodie sighed and pulled the door open. "You scared me to death! I thought you were that woman."

Maddie nodded toward the others in the room and set a dish on the table. "Here's a casserole for supper." She wrung her hands together nervously. "I'm afraid I have some more bad news." She hesitated. "Your mother passed away a couple of hours ago." She reached for Jodie's hand. "I'm sorry, child. I know she wasn't the best mother, but I'm sure you had feelings for her."

141

Jodie couldn't believe it, although she knew it could happen, she just didn't think it would. She didn't like her mom, but she sure didn't wish death upon her. "Her liver?" she asked.

"Yes, dear."

Carlos wrapped his arms around Jodie's shoulder and squeezed. "I'm sorry."

"Me, too," said Tara.

"It's my fault, Maddie."

"It's not your fault, Jodanne. Why would you say such a thing?"

"I thought Snake killed Nicole. I tried to confront him, but he reached for his gun, and I shot him in the leg. He retaliated by shooting my mother. And now I find out that he had nothing to do with Nicole's disappearance!" Jodie bowed her head. "This mess is my fault."

"Child, it's not your fault. You're mother died because she had a bad liver. The alcohol is what killed her. So don't you dare be blaming yourself for this!"

"What do I do now? What will happen to me?" She didn't cry, although she was terribly depressed. It was the worst feeling. She'd been so sad about Nicole, but she didn't miss her mother like that, only the thought of losing her mother, which was bizarre. Although her mother was a horrible person, at least she'd had a mother. Now she really was all alone in the world—first Nicole and now her mother. Who would be next? She glanced toward Carlos and Tara as a sinking feeling besieged her.

"I'm not sure what needs to be done. I don't know what to do about a burial. If you come forward, they'll know you're around." Maddie shook her head and folded her arms across her chest. "This is terrible to say, but you might just have to let the state take care of her remains."

Carlos's eyes locked with Jodie's. "If you don't, you'll be put into foster care."

"I don't care about any funeral. We'll just go on pretending I can't be found." Jodie glanced toward Tara. "Be sure to tell Taylor that you couldn't find me today."

"You can stay with me," Maddie said.

"Thanks, Maddie, but that would be the first placed they looked." She dropped down in the recliner. "I just need the evening to think this through."

"Sure, I'll go now. If you need me, I'll be home." She turned back. "You doing okay with money?"

"Yes, thanks."

Maddie acted as if she wanted to say more—but didn't.

Jodie could have sworn there were tears in Maddie's eyes, which she rarely witnessed. "I'll be fine, Maddie."

"Okay, child. Stop by tomorrow." Her eyes locked with Carlos. "Take care of her."

"I will, I promise," Carlos opened the door for her.

Tara stood and retrieved the keys from her purse. "I'm really sorry, Jodie. I know God will help you get through this."

"What?" Jodie grimaced. "You mean the same God that helped you get through your parents death by allowing you to be attacked by a thug and then shot at?"

Tara placed her hands on her hip. "That's not fair."

"Maybe not, but it's true."

"I'm still alive because of God," Tara stuttered. "Jodie, life's not fair, but God is good."

"You're crazy."

"Okay, girls," Carlos interrupted, "now is not the time to be arguing."

"Sorry, but I do have a few problems to deal with," Jodie snapped.

"Hey, I'm on your side. I'm here to help." Carlos grabbed her hand, but she pulled it away.

"You know, I appreciate all you two have done, but I think I need some alone time."

"Now you're mad." Carlos said softly.

"I need to get home anyway." Tara walked toward the door. "I guess you won't be going to school tomorrow."

"No." Jodie hesitated. "Would you drop off a report to Mr. Bobbit's class? It's due tomorrow." She walked over to the kitchen table and fumbled through the pile of papers.

"Yeah, sure."

Jodie found the report and handed it to Tara. "I'm sorry for yelling at you. I'm just not dealing with the situation too well."

"Sure, I understand. I'll come by tomorrow after school. Taylor's dad offered to give me a ride home from school and help us if we need it."

"Oh... okay." Jodie thought that was an odd thing for a stranger to do, but it was Taylor's dad, so his intentions must be good.

Tara left, and Jodie spun around to face Carlos. "I really need to be alone."

"I'm not leaving you. You *don't* need to be alone."

"Carlos, I'm sorry, but that's exactly what I do *need.*"

"You know, it's okay to cry."

She was irritated now. "I don't want to cry! I want to be left alone, dammit!"

"Okay, okay." He threw up his hands as he backed away from her. He shrugged, grabbed his bag off the table, and hurried toward the door.

"I'm sorry," Jodie called out, but he didn't reply.

The sound of the door slamming was the only response she got.

The tears surfaced. He was the last person she wanted to piss off, but it was too late now. She locked the door, set the casserole in the fridge, and then collapsed on the couch. She couldn't believe all that had happened.

The tears finally came. She hadn't wanted the others to see her tearing up.

She missed Nicole terribly, and now she wondered *if it was J.J.* that was hiding something. She figured he probably knew more than he was admitting. Nicole had been missing almost a week, and Jodie was sure her chances of being found alive were slim.

After a while, the tears ceased, and she blew her nose.

She glanced toward her mom's bedroom. There would be no more strange men in there or loud offensive noises awakening her throughout the night. She slowly walked toward the bedroom

144

door. She stood in the archway, staring at the unmade bed and clothes spewed out over the chair. She hesitated and then stepped into the room. A sudden chill filled her bones, and the urge to turn around and run overwhelmed her. She swallowed and forced herself to circle the bed, running her hand along the silk sheets. At one point, she glanced down, not realizing she'd twisted the sheet into a knot and was yanking furiously on it. She immediately released the sheet and stepped away from the bed. She hadn't been in the room for ages, and blocked memories were starting to surface. Goosebumps suddenly emerged, and she quickly glanced behind her. For a split second, Jodie wondered if it was possible that the doctor read the report wrong on her mom, and it had said *released* instead of *deceased*. She quickly dismissed the silly notion.

She stared at the closed closet door for the longest moment, debating. She slowly strolled toward it. Her breath quickened, and her hand trembled as she grasped the doorknob. *You don't have to do this*, she told herself.

She didn't hesitate—she flung the door open and frantically searched through the hanging clothes, not sure exactly what she was looking for.

She gasped as her eyes settled on the wool scarves at the back of the closet. They were just like she remembered them—one was a vintage gray, which always reminded her of something an elderly patient in a nursing home would wear, the other one was a dark red like the color of fresh blood, it was worn-looking and tattered. *These shouldn't be here! Why are they still here?* She jerked the scarves off the hangers and tossed them to the floor.

She suddenly dropped to her knees and doubled over as the images came flooding back. She covered her ears as Nicole's screams pierced her memory. Nicole was ten years old, and mother was furious because she'd forgotten to put the toothpaste back in the drawer. Mother stripped away Nicole's clothes and tied her face down to the bed with the scarves. Her mother made Jodie count the number of times she whipped Nicole with the leather belt. Jodie had cowered in the corner of the room, crying, as the whelps emerged over Nicole's backside. Jodie pleaded

145

with her mother to stop, but her mother only laughed and threatened she'd be next if she stopped counting. Thirty two times Jodie counted! Her mother had picked that number because it was the number of men she'd been with that year. Jodie would never forget that number for as long as she lived.

She recalled how Nicole could hardly walk afterwards, and how she'd doctored her back every night for a week. Nicole had made her pinky swear she'd never tell a sole about the incident. And Jodie never did. All these years Jodie had been ashamed of what her mother had done to them. She'd grown up believing the beatings were their fault.

"You bitch! I hate you!" Jodie screamed. She beat her fists wildly against the wood floor. "I'm glad you're dead!" She jumped to her feet and shoved everything on the dresser onto the floor. She ran to the kitchen, pulled open a drawer, and grabbed the scissors. She ran back into the bedroom and shredded the scarves as other horrid memories surfaced. She snatched the lamp off the end table and flung it across the room, shattering the base of it. "You can't hurt me any more!"

She suddenly glanced upwards. *Maybe, there was a God after all.*

Chapter Sixteen

Tara was so furious she could spit! *How could Jodie not believe in God?* She tossed her books on the table and retrieved the milk from the refrigerator. She'd been speechless and couldn't think of anything of value to argue back with her. All she could come up with was the quote that her pastor always used, *'Life is not fair, but God is good.'* She hadn't thought of that saying for so long, at least not since her parents were killed. If only she could convince Jodie of God, but she didn't know how to do it. If Jodie had some faith, maybe she wouldn't give up on life so easily. Although Tara knew there were people that didn't believe in God, she personally never knew one that didn't. She just assumed that most people believed.

She suddenly blamed Sheila. It wasn't Jodie's fault she didn't know anything about God or Jesus. It was her mother's fault for not teaching her or taking her to church. She said a quick prayer for Jodie and poured the milk in a glass.

The earlier incident was still fresh on her mind. She couldn't believe that Taylor and her father pulled up at the time that they did. She knew it wasn't just a coincidence—God had heard her prayers again. She drank the milk and then laid her head down on the table.

How much longer could she live like this? It seemed like every day was a game of survival. She knew life was supposed to be challenging, but this was ridiculous! Life shouldn't be this difficult.

Tara jerked her head up as the key in the lock turned. Tommy stumbled in, dropping a sack of groceries on the couch as he passed.

She glanced toward the clock. "What are you doing home this early?"

"I took off early because I had some things I needed to wrap up with the lawyer." He glanced around the room as if he was surprised everything was still in order. "Get cleaned up," he said excitedly.

"Why?"

"We're celebrating! We're going out." He rubbed his hands together. "We got the apartment. We'll be moving next week!"

"You're kidding me?"

"No." He nodded. "It's true."

She jumped up and wrapped her arms around his neck. "Oh, Tommy, you're the best." She was going to tell him about Snake, but since they were so close to getting out of the neighborhood, it could wait until after the move.

"What do you feel like? Pizza?" Tommy asked.

"That sounds yummy to me! I'll just change my shirt, and I'll be ready." Suddenly she remembered Jodie. "Oh, I got bad news."

A sudden crease emerged across Tommy's forehead. "What happened, now?"

"Don't worry; it's not me this time. It's Jodie—her mother died today."

"Oh, wow." He pulled out the kitchen chair and sat. "That poor girl. Well, if her mom was as mean as you say she was, maybe it was a blessing in disguise."

"But what will happen to her now?" she asked.

"I'm sure a relative will take her in."

"She doesn't have any."

"None?"

"Just a sister that is nowhere to be found."

Tommy massaged his temples. "I really don't know. Since she's still under age I guess the authorities will take over."

"She won't go."

148

"I'm afraid she won't have a choice."

"I know Jodie, she'll run away first. She said there's too much abuse going on in foster care."

"Well, surely it can't be any worse than what she's already been through."

"She seems to think so." Tara strolled to the window and stared out. "I'm really worried about her."

"I'm sure you are. She's been a good friend to you." He stood. "Well, go get dressed, and we'll talk over dinner. I'll have to think on this one."

Tara grabbed a shirt and hurried to the restroom. As thrilled as she was about moving, her heart was breaking for Jodie. She couldn't just run off and leave her to fend for herself. Although she'd only known her for a few weeks, she'd grown close to her. She knew if Jodie remained in her apartment or her hideout, Snake would eventually catch up with her.

Suddenly, reality came crashing back as the earlier incident reminded her that her own life was still at risk.

She pulled the shirt over her head and ran a brush through her hair.

She knew she wasn't out of danger yet, and the survival game wouldn't end until she was out of this neighborhood!

***

Jodie's sleep was deep and her dream was surreal. She was in this huge square room, standing in a long line. Everything was white, including the furniture. She wasn't sure why she was waiting in line. She just knew every few seconds someone would disappear behind the big gold-framed doors and never come back out. Everyone seemed excited and anxious to get through the doors.

Finally, it was her turn. She slowly swung open the doors and entered. It was dark at first, but the further she walked the lighter it grew until the sun was suddenly beaming brightly above her. There were fresh sunflowers and daisies floating in the air. She sniffed—the sweet aroma soothed her. She curled

149

her toes on the plush green grass beneath her feet and giggled. She held out her hands and spun around several times. She was so happy. She didn't know why she felt so good, but she didn't want the feeling to ever end.

And then she saw her, flying through the air. Nicole's red hair whipped against her back as she bounced from one cloud to another. She wore a beautiful blue sequin gown with white pearls, and a chain made of daisies encircled her neck and wrists. She floated freely through the air as if she'd been doing it her whole life. Jodie called out to her, but she didn't respond.

Nicole grabbed another girl's hand, and they laughed and jumped up and down on a cotton-like cloud.

Jodie screamed her name as loud as she could, but she still didn't acknowledge her.

Suddenly the room turned pitch black and a huge figure emerge from the darkness. Jodie was so frightened she fell to her knees and covered her head.

She slowly lifted her eyes. Evil faces with horns and no bodies floated around the room. Jodie cringed—they were bloodcurdling. Their eyes were on the outside of their faces and their lips were tucked inside of their mouths.

The happy feeling had vanished and now she was terrified. She cowered backwards, but the figure loomed in front of her. "Why are you here?" he said.

Jodie tried to see his face, but her eyes suddenly burned. "I want to be with my sister. I saw her just a minute ago. Please take me to my sister."

"Only the ones that believe get to go in that room, the rest stay in this room!"

"Oh no, I can't... I can't stay here. I believe... I do, I do..." The figure disappeared and the appalling faces surrounded her, taunting her. She screamed into the darkness, "Don't leave me...please don't leave me here."

Suddenly Jodie stirred awake with the dream fresh on her mind. It was a horrible dream, and she just wanted to forget it quickly. She suddenly grew still. As horrifying as the dream was, she knew she didn't wake because of it. Something else had wakened her. She listened. Although the room was too dark to see anything, she had an eerie felling that she wasn't alone. *There it was...that sound again.* She slowly turned her ear toward the bedroom door. She immediately recognized faint breathing, as if someone was trying hard not to breathe. *Was it Snake back for more retaliation?* Her adrenaline increased as her mouth grew dry. *Had she forgot to lock up?* No, she was certain that she had. She remained lying on her side and slowly slid her hand to the side of the mattress, knowing it was impossible to reach the pistol from the position she was in. She hoped the recent dream wasn't an indication of what the future had in store for her. Her body trembled as she contemplated what to do. She could jump up and try to reach the gun before her assailant killed her. She was certain her chances were slim to impossible for succeeding. The only other thing she could do was to try to bluff her way out.

She cocked her head forward and waited. A feather-like step caused the floorboard to squeak and that was enough to confirm her suspicious. Jodie bolted straight up, stuck her hands under the cover, and pointed it into the air. "I am going to blow your friggen head off if you take another step."

"Don't shoot, Jodie." The light flickered on, and Nicole stood wide-eyed in the doorway, grasping a piece of paper. "I was just leaving you a note." She shook the paper above her head.

Jodie rubbed her eyes. She thought she was still dreaming. "Nicole?" She jumped to her feet and ran to her. She hugged her tightly. "Where have you been?" The tears tumbled off her cheeks. "I thought you were dead."

"I'm sorry, Jodie. I didn't mean to scare you." She glanced nervously behind her. "I only have a few minutes so sit down, and I'll explain." She glanced around the room as if she was seeing it for the first time. "I heard about mother. Are you sad?"

"No. Are you?"

"Not at all. She was a vicious woman."

"Did J.J. hurt you? Because if he did, I'll make him pay?"

"No, Jodie. J.J.'s not responsible for what I've done. This was my idea. I ran away with a man I fell in love with."

151

Jodie, dazed, ran her hand through her hair. "What? What are you talking about?"

"I'm so sorry I did this to you, but I couldn't let you know because I knew J.J. would come looking for me, and if you knew something, he would have made you talk."

"So you staged all of this? You made me think you were hurt or *dead*! *And J.J. did have a hand in this*—he had Randy killed because he thought he was involved." She paced to the other side of the room. She spun around. "I can't believe you did this to me."

"J.J. killed Randy because he was dealing on his turf. I think he's known about it for a while. I should have told you, so you could have warned Randy. I'm sorry." She sighed. "I know I shouldn't have done what I done, but I didn't have any choice. It's the only way I could..."

"Wait a minute. What about your picture? Someone broke in here and took your picture off the dresser."

Nicole bowed her head. "That was me, too," she said softly. "I had to make you think someone else had abducted me in case J.J. started harassing you. I was trying to protect you."

"Protect me? Actually, you almost got me killed." Jodie threw her hands up in the air. "First, I confronted J.J. myself, and I thought he was going to kill me, and if that wasn't enough, I challenged a gang member and then shot him because I thought he was holding out information."

"I am so sorry, Jodie."

Jodie hurried toward the dresser, pulled out a drawer, and held up the diary. "And what about this and the missing pages? Was the *real* truth on the missing pages? And then you sugar-coated how happy you were with J.J. on the pages you left intact?" She tossed the diary on the bed. "I should have caught on. I knew you wouldn't talk highly of J.J. like you did."

"I wrote what I did in hopes that J.J. would find the diary and believe that foul play was the reason for my disappearance. I never meant to hurt you." A single tear slid down Nicole's face. "I had to get away from him, and I didn't know any other way. I knew he'd kill me if he found out I'd escaped."

152

Jodie caught a glimpse of her own reflection in the mirror. Her hair was messy and sticking up in places that it normally didn't, and her face was as red as a fire hydrant. *Yeah, because I'm mad as hell,* she thought silently. She imagined her blood pressure was sky high. She inhaled a deep breath. "So what now? Did you come back to rescue me now that mom is gone?"

"Well?" Jodie didn't give Nicole time to respond. "So, where is the hero that saved you?"

"Jodie, I love you more than anything, but I didn't come back here to get you." She grabbed her hand. "I only came back to leave you the note and to let you know I was okay."

Jodie's eyebrow's furrowed. "I don't understand?" Her words pieced her heart. "What am I supposed to do now?"

"I'm so sorry, but I'm afraid Jeremy wouldn't allow it."

"What do you mean?" Jodie yelled. "If he loves you, he'll understand. Just tell him you have a sister that doesn't have anywhere to go because you're mother's dead, or else she's going to be put in foster care." She glared at her. "You do remember all the stories we've heard about foster care, don't you?"

"Of course I do, and I remember that our life wasn't much easier, either!" Nicole wiped the tears away with a tissue. "You know, I'd take you with me if I could?"

"What kind of asshole did you fall in love with?" Jodie's eyes suddenly widened, and her mouth dropped opened. "He's another pimp, isn't he?"

Nicole looked away.

"I don't believe this! What were you thinking?" Jodie wondered if Nicole's surprises would ever end. "You got away from one pimp to go to another?"

"I didn't know he was. And I do think he really loves me." She paused. "He's not mean like J.J." Another pause. "I just didn't know there were other girls."

Jodie fought the urge to shake her sister. As pissed as she was, she couldn't help but feel sorry for Nicole. Her eyes were sad-looking and the dark circles underneath them aged her once youthful face. Jodie thought she could easily pass for twenty-five or older. "Where are you living?"

"In Trenton, New Jersey." She looked down at her watch. "I really need to go—he's outside waiting. I had to beg him to bring me here."

Jodie swallowed. "Sure, if you have to go." She walked her to the door. "When will I see you again?"

"I don't know." She hugged Jodie. "But I promise we'll see each other again." She reached for a tissue and blew her nose. "I'm so sorry I can't help you! I really do love you and miss you."

"I know. I'll be fine." She watched Nicole scurry down the hall, and then she cursed under her breath and slammed the door! She'd stayed composed in front of her because she didn't want Nicole to see how weak she was slowly becoming. But inside she was dying! She'd wanted to scream at Nicole and beg to go with her, but she hadn't.

Although she was thankful that Nicole was still alive, she was furious with her. She couldn't believe she could just walk out of her life like she'd done. Jodie knew she'd never see her again. She was certain that Nicole didn't want to ever be found because she didn't leave any contact information. *And she says she loves me?* Jodie wondered what life would have been like if she'd contacted the police to bring Nicole back home when she'd first ran away. The main reason Jodie had tried to better herself through school was, that one day, she'd planned to save Nicole. But apparently, Nicole didn't feel the same way about her.

Jodie clinched her fists and fought the urge to scream. She sat at the table and sobbed. She knew life would never be the same again. And the worst part was she didn't have a clue what to do about it. She didn't want to go to foster care, but if she didn't, she'd have to quit school. And if she quit school, she'd probably end up in the same position Nicole was in. After another long hour of sulking, she flipped the TV on and stared at the screen. But the sound of pleasant voices just depressed her more, and she quickly flipped it off. She stared into the kitchen toward the cabinets for the longest time. Finally, she jumped to her feet and searched every cabinet until she found what she was looking for. She grabbed the bottle of liquor and quickly opened it. The first drink burnt like hell, but after a few sips, it slid down easier. She waited for the numb feeling to come. She wanted to forget everything. She wanted to die!

Chapter Seventeen

Tara thanked Taylor and her father for the ride, and jumped out of the car. She was so grateful they had volunteered to give her a ride home from school. And she was thrilled it was Friday, and in just a few days, she'd be out of the horrid neighborhood and away from Snake forever. She carefully scanned the hallway before entering into the building. She still needed to be cautious though. She was certain Snake was furious about yesterday. She knew from experience that he didn't take defeat easily.

She twisted the key in the lock and leaped inside. She threw her bag on the couch and hurried toward the refrigerator. She poured a glass of milk and downed half of it in one swallow. She was eager to change clothes and get to Jodie's. She had some good news that she was eager to deliver. While they were having Pizza last night, Tommy suggested that he try to get custody of Jodie. Tara hadn't made any comments through dinner to influence his decision. She certainly didn't argue it, but she hadn't been the one to bring it up, either. She decided that Tommy was just an all-around good person! She was so fortunate to have him as an uncle. He told her that not only did her parents leave enough money for her to go to college, but they also left a generous amount for him to take care of her. He said he didn't know if he could make it happen with Jodie, but he'd try.

Tara had been so excited last night that she didn't know if she could wait to tell Jodie. She wanted to run over and tell her as soon as they got home, but she knew Jodie needed space to deal with her mom's death and all that was happening, so she decided to wait until today.

A knock on the door interrupted her thoughts. Her heartbeat quickened, and for a brief second, she thought of *Snake*. She quickly dismissed the thought because knocking on doors wasn't his style. It had to be Jodie. She tiptoed quietly to peek out the hole. She sighed and pulled the door open. "Hey, Carlos. What's up? Where's Jodie?"

"Are you busy? Can I talk to you?"

"Sure. Come on in."

Carlos followed Tara into the living room and paced nervously in front of the couch. "I just left Jodie's." He clinched his hands into fists, flexed his fingers back out, and popped his knuckles.

Tara had never seen Carlos so flustered. "Yeah. Is she okay?"

"She wants to break up?"

"What? Why would she do that? I know she likes you."

"I'm not sure. I got mad at her last night and stormed out, but I didn't think she'd still be mad today."

"No, Jodie's not one to hold a grudge. She got mad at me yesterday too, but I didn't think anything of it."

Carlos ran his hand nervously through his hair. "Then I don't know what it is. I thought we had something good going between us." His glossy eyes traveled to the window. "You know, I really like her."

"I know you do. It's probably just this thing with her mom and not knowing what's going to happen to her."

"And I think she's drinking. I could smell it on her."

"That's not good." Her heart went out for Carlos. He looked like he was going to break any second. She would have never guessed him to be so sensitive. "Well, I got some news for her that might lift her spirits. My uncle is going to try to get custody of her. I was on my way over to tell her."

"That's great. I didn't sleep last night from worrying about her. I didn't want to leave her, especially with that friggen thug

157

still roaming around. I should have insisted I stayed, but she wanted to be left alone."

"I'll try talking to her. Just give her some time. She's troubled right now, but she'll come around."

"Thanks. I'd appreciate it. I'm not going to bug her any more today." He moved toward the door. "Will you keep an eye on her?"

"I will, and I'll have her come stay the night with me."

"Okay. Maybe I should leave her alone for a couple of days. Give her time to miss me, you know?" He winked.

Tara was glad he still had his sense of humor. "I think that might be what she needs. No offense, of course."

"None taken. Thanks, Tara." He pulled his wallet out and flipped out a business card. "Here's my work number, and my cell number is on there, too. If anything comes up, anything at all, promise, you'll give me a call?"

"I will." Tara shut the door and hurried to change. She was shocked that Jodie had broken up with Carlos. She was certain something else was going on.

A few minutes later she was standing in front of Jodie's door, knocking. "Jodie, it's me."

The door flew open. "Come in." Jodie stepped over a pile of shoes on the floor and pulled a trash sack out of a box.

Tara scanned the living room; it was a mess. There were piles of clothes scattered on the floor, a half dozen full trash sacks were setting near the door. "What are you doing?"

"Getting rid of my old life!"

"You're throwing out your mother's things?"

"And Nicole's!"

"Nicole's? But why? You're not giving up your search for her, are you?"

"No need to search for her. She was here last night. She's fine. She just found a new pimp to cater to!"

"Omigod!" Now Tara understood why Jodie had broken up with Carlos. It had nothing to do with her mother—it was Nicole. "Tell me what happened."

158

Jodie picked up a half-filled glass off the coffee table and downed it. She poured the remaining liquor from the bottle into the glass. She sighed, shoved a bundle of clothes over, and parked herself on the couch. She quickly filled Tara in on the details from the night before.

Tara shook her head in disbelief. "Wow, what a shock!" No wonder Jodie's eyes were swollen and blood shot. She'd probably been up all night, crying. She glanced toward the empty liquor bottle. She'd almost commented on her drinking—she was glad she hadn't—under the circumstances anyway. "What are you going to do with all their stuff?"

"Trash it."

Tara glanced toward the high heels on the floor. "You could probably sell some of this stuff and make a little money."

Jodie nursed her drink while thumping her fingers against the glass. "I just want to get rid of it as fast as I can. I only have to the end of May to vacate this place."

"Well, I do have some good news. Tommy said he was going to try to get custody of you, so you don't have to go to foster care." She waited for some kind of reaction from Jodie—when there was none, she continued, "You'll finally get out of this neighborhood. There's an extra bedroom in the apartment for you, also." She paused. "Isn't that great?"

"Yeah, sure." Jodie stood and walked to the window. "I'm sorry, I don't mean to sound ungrateful. Thank Tommy for me, but I don't think they will grant him custody. If they won't grant Maddie custody, they're not going to grant custody to a single man that is already raising his niece."

"You never know—they might. Anyway, he's going to talk to his lawyer today."

A tear slid down Jodie's cheek and she quickly flicked away. "You know bad luck has followed me all through my life, why should it change now?" She gazed out the window. "I've accepted it—there's no destiny for me. And I really don't care any more." She walked back to the coffee table, picked up her drink, and sipped.

159

"Don't talk like that, Jodie." Tara paused. "You can go to my house tonight and stay. You don't need to be alone, especially with Snake still out there, plotting his retaliation!"

Jodie settled back on the couch. "Thanks, but I'm going to stay here during the day and hide out at my spot at night. It's warm enough now. There's no room for me at your uncles anyway."

"We'll make room." Tara could tell the alcohol was affecting Jodie's speech, her words were slurring together.

"Thanks, but I need some time alone right now. I'll just come back here during the daytime."

"That gives me the willies to think you'll be sleeping in that hole during the night."

"It's not like I never done it before. I'll be fine—don't worry."

"What happened with you and Carlos? I could have swore you were nuts about him."

"I do like him, but he deserves better." She finished her drink, slammed the glass down, and picked up the empty bottle. "Damn, I might have to go to Chester's tonight."

"How can you drink that stuff?"

"Haven't you ever heard of *'like daughter like mother'* or maybe it's *'like mother like daughter.'* Anyway, I am my mother's child and her bad habits were bound to influence me one day. I can't control who I am."

Tara had never heard Jodie talk like that—it was as if she was giving up on everything. She was sure it was the alcohol. "But *you* can. Your life is not over, Jodie."

"It might as well as be. I'll never amount to anything anyway. My mother's right, you know, I can still hear her saying, *'you ain't ever going to amount to shit'.* You know she used to say that a lot."

"Your mother had problems."

"Yeah...me!" She stood and shrugged. "Listen to me, feeling sorry for myself. I hate people that do that, and now, I'm doing it." She strolled to the kitchen and tossed the empty bottle in the trashcan.

160

"You have every right to be depressed. You have been through a lot this last week. I still get depressed over my parents, but I'm not giving up on life. They wouldn't want me to."

"If it was up to my mother—she'd prefer I was the one that was shot."

Tara remained silent; she knew Jodie was right.

"I hate to be rude, but I think I'm going to shower and get out of this place for awhile."

"Jodie, I don't know…what about Snake."

"I'm tired of living in fear because of him. I'm in no mood for him…besides I'll have my pistol."

"I don't think Tommy will let me out of the apartment after dark."

"You don't have to come. I'm a big girl." She walked to the door and opened it. "I have no one to answer to anymore."

Tara glanced toward the open door. "I guess that's a hint that I should leave." She walked toward the door. "Promise me, you'll be careful."

"I'll be fine. Don't worry. Maybe, I'll see you tomorrow."

"I'll let you know what Tommy finds out."

"Okay, tell him thanks."

Tara hurried down the hallway, keeping her eyes alert. She ran across the street and dashed into her own apartment.

She was concerned about Jodie, especially with all the drinking lately. It was so unlike her. She just wasn't acting the same. She glanced out the window. Before long, it would be dark, and Snake would be out there, lurking in the shadows. Even though Jodie's mom was dead, she was certain that Snake wasn't satisfied yet.

***

Jodie stared blankly at the glass in front of her. Jack hadn't wanted to serve her, but she easily convinced him that she wasn't drunk, although her head was pounding. She knew she didn't need another drink, but she couldn't stop. If she allowed her brain to function normally, then the events from the night before

161

would surface. And she couldn't allow herself to feel that pain again. She wanted to forget about Nicole forever. This was the lowest she'd ever felt in her life.

"Come on, Jodie, one game," Bronze yelled from the back of the bar.

Jodie slid off the bar stool, grabbed her drink, and made her way to the back. "Sorry, bud, but no pool for me tonight."

"You're scared I'm going to beat you, aren't you?"

"You bet I am, and I'm not going to let you ruin my undefeated title just because I'm drinking."

"You wuss!" Bronze laughed.

Matt tossed his pool stick on the table. "What, you getting tired of me whipping your ass?" he asked Bronze.

"Shut up! You're just getting lucky." Bronze pulled up a chair next to Jodie. "So Jodie, I haven't seen you stumbling around like this for quite some time. What's the occasion?"

"I'm not stumbling."

"You're drunk," Matt added.

"I'm not drunk—I just got a little buzz." Jodie sipped her drink. She'd been drinking most of the day off and on. She did manage to take a short nap before she came to Chester's, which helped sober her up for a short time. She snarled her nose as the liquor slid down her throat. The smell was starting to get to her. She placed her hand over her stomach as the queasiness increased. Suddenly, she jumped to her feet, covered her mouth, and ran to the restroom.

A few minutes later, she returned to the table with her hand over her stomach. "Oh crap, I feel horrible.

Bronze grinned. "Can I buy you a drink, Flipper?"

She flipped him the bird.

"Leave her alone, Bronze. I can remember not to long ago when you were shit-faced," Matt said.

"I know, I know...but Flip never gets drunk—it's a nice switch!" His gaze shifted to the front of the bar. "Well, look who just came in."

162

Jodie followed his gaze. "Oh, shit... Carlos." She quickly turned away, but it was too late, he'd seen her.

"Back here," Bronze shouted.

Jodie rolled her eyes. "Thanks, Bronze."

"Why? What's up with you and Carlos?"

"I'm just not in the mood to be lectured." She turned toward Matt. "Will you give me a ride home?"

Carlos reached the table before Matt could respond. "Hey, guys." His eyes shifted to Jodie. "Jodie, can we talk?"

"Tonight's not good for me. Matt was just going to give me a ride home, weren't you, Matt?"

"Whenever," Matt shrugged.

"Are you drunk, Jodie?" Carlos eyes narrowed.

"What if I am," she snapped.

Carlos nudged Matt. "Come on. I'll ride with you guys."

Jodie rolled her eyes and followed Matt out the door, keeping a few feet in front of Carlos. As much as she tried not to stagger, a few times she caught herself swaying to the left. She hated Carlos seeing her this way.

As they neared the car Carlos grabbed Jodie's elbow and twirled her around. "What is going on with you? What the hell did I do to you?"

"Nothing."

"Then why are you treating me this way?"

Jodie tried not to waver, but he was so close to her. Just the scent of his cologne made her want to wrap her arms around his neck and beg him to help her. But she couldn't. She wouldn't ask that of him. She straightened her back and responded in a flat tone, "We just don't have anything in common, Carlos. We weren't meant to be together." She bowed her head to avoid the hurt in his eyes.

He lifted her chin. "Do you really mean that?"

"Of course I do," she stuttered. Although she wanted to scream, *I'm lying, you idiot, can't you see that.* "You really don't need to ride with us. I'll be fine."

He stared at her for the longest time, as though he was trying to figure out the meaning of her words. Finally, he spoke, "Okay,

163

Jodie, if that's the way you really feel, I'll leave you alone." He rubbed his hands together as if to indicate he was done with her. He spun on his heels and went back inside Chester's.

She stared after him. *What had she done? She didn't mean it! It was the alcohol talking!* She started to chase after him, but she couldn't. She cared about him too much. She couldn't drag him down with her.

All her life she'd fought to be normal. She'd faced poverty, being abused, and daily peer pressure, but none of it compared to the despair she felt now. She spun back around toward Matt, who was casually leaning against the car, shaking his head. "Don't say anything, just take me home."

All she wanted was to climb into her warm bed.

She cursed silently—she couldn't go home. It was too dangerous. She'd have Matt drop her off in the alley and wait while she dashed to her hideaway. She hoped she didn't fall through the window while trying to climb through.

She climbed in the car, threw her head back against the headrest, and closed her eyes. At least the spinning stopped. Memories of the night before came rushing back. She squeezed her eyes tighter shut, so the tears wouldn't come. *Nicole, please come home*, she said silently.

Chapter Eighteen

Tara stretched her arms toward the ceiling and arched her feet upwards, and then she pointed them toward the end of the couch, stretching her legs at the same time. She was once told it was beneficial to stretch your muscles in the morning before getting up. The concept had stuck, and she'd been doing it ever since. She stood and did a quick twist with her waist. She was glad it was Saturday.

It wasn't quite nine yet, but she'd promised Tommy she'd do some of the packing, so she wanted to get an early start. He'd brought home a dozen boxes yesterday for her to get started. It was going to be a busy day, but first, she needed to run over to Jodie's and let her know what Tommy's lawyer had said. He'd said they just needed to tell the court that Jodie was living with them before her mother died, and they would probably grant Tommy custody.

She was so excited. Now there wasn't any reason in the world for Jodie to want to stick around here *except for Maddie*. She knew it would be hard for Jodie to leave her. Maddie was like a grandma to Jodie. That part would be difficult, but if Jodie didn't agree to live with her and Tommy, she'd be put in foster care and wouldn't be near Maddie anyway.

Tara quickly changed and hurried toward the window to check the weather. The sun was brightly shining through. She pulled open the window and stuck her arm out. The heat from the sun warmed her insides, and the lukewarm wind was

165

refreshing. She smiled—glad that the cold winter months were behind them. She hated wearing sweaters and jackets. Although she was thin, they always made her feel bulky.

A robin flew on a telephone line, chirping contentedly as if to say he was happy to be alive. She gazed down at the bushes that were already green and full. Some red and yellow tulips had bloomed in a patch down the street. She never thought that this part of the city could be beautiful, but spring had that effect on everything it touched. She inhaled deeply and let it out. "What, no smog," she mumbled. It was going to be a glorious day!

Her eyes shifted toward a silver car cruising down the street. *What was it that was so familiar?* She got a glimpse of the driver, and the red headband around his head suddenly triggered her memory. She hit the floor with a thug. How could she have forgotten the silver Oldsmobile that had carried the gang members that had tried to kill her? "Omigod, not again." She said a quick prayer, and trembling, she pulled herself toward the edge of the window. She held her breath and slowly peeked over the ledge. The car was already down the street and turning the corner.

She stood and glanced up and down the street. She was certain that Snake was a passenger in the car. But his intentions had her puzzled. Why would he be in the neighborhood this early in the morning? Whatever the reason, she was certain he was up to no good.

She grabbed her purse and keys, and rushed out the door. She was glad the sidewalks were bustling with people in case he decided to come back.

She hurried across the street into Jodie's building. She darted down the hallway, jumping when Maddie's door flew opened.

"Well, child, it sounds like a herd of elephants running down the hall. What's your hurry?" Maddie asked.

"Sorry, Maddie. I'm on my way to see Jodie. I have great news."

"I need to talk to her myself. Hang on for just a second, and I'll go with you." She crossed the room and scooped up a platter covered with foil. "I got fried chicken for lunch. There's plenty for you, too."

"It's smells wonderful. I don't know when I had fried chicken last." Her eyes clouded over. "Yeah I do, it was the night before my parents were killed. Mom had fried chicken and mashed potatoes with gravy and baked homemade rolls." She smiled at the memory. "She was a good cook."

Maddie wrapped her arm around Tara's shoulders as she guided her down the hall. "I'm sure she was, child." She squeezed Tara. "It's good for you to talk about the memories. Don't ever let them build up inside. It's good therapy to talk about your losses."

"Do you still talk about your son?"

"Girl, I ask God about Jerome every day. I even catch myself telling him the same stories over and over." She winked. "I know God already knows the stories, but I like to tell them, all the same, and he is the best listener, you know?"

"Yes, I know. Maddie, how did you get to be such a good person?"

They reached Jodie's door and Tara knocked.

"I believe we are all born good. It's just the paths we choose to follow that changes us," Maddie said.

"That makes sense." She pounded again on Jodie's door. "Jodie, it's me."

"I hope she's okay," Maddie said. "I've been worried about her."

After several seconds, the door slowly opened, and Jodie stood, speechless. Her face was streaked with tears, and mascara was smudged underneath her eyes. Tara recognized the shirt and jeans as the same she'd had on the day before except the shirt was wrinkled now. She knew something was terribly wrong, and it only took a glance around the room to realize what Jodie was so upset about. The room had been trashed. The couch cushions had been slit and stuffing scattered all over the floor. The chair had been flipped over and shivers of smashed glass covered the floor. The TV was gone along with the lamps.

Maddie quickly set the platter on the kitchen table and gathered Jodie in her arms. "Jodanne, are you okay? What happened? Did anyone hurt you?"

Jodie couldn't quit sobbing long enough to answer.

While Maddie was consoling Jodie, Tara strolled through the rest of the apartment. It was in shambles, too. The bathroom water must have been left on because the floor was soaked. The medicine cabinet had been ransacked and unwanted medications were scattered everywhere. She closed the cabinet door, picked the medicine off the floor, and piled them next to the sink. She gathered some towels out of the linen closet and spread them out on the floor to soak up the water. She had a feeling every room was going to be a disaster. She ducked into Jodie's bedroom next. The mattresses were sliced, the blankets shredded and everything on the dressers was knocked to the floor. But what really caught her attention were the words scribbled across Jodie's mirror, K JODIE. "Ohmigod," she said aloud, "Is that blood?" She stared dumbfounded at the scribble words, which she was certain was done in blood. No wonder Jodie was devastated. Snake had come here to kill her.

She shivered and ran her hands up and down her arms. They had to go to the police. This was getting out of control. Somehow, she was going to have to convince Jodie. "No," she said sharply. They couldn't do that because then they would know Jodie was living alone. She shook her head. She didn't know what to do. Maybe Tommy would know. She poked her head in Sheila's room and it was in no better condition. She moved back into the living room where Jodie was still crying hysterically.

"I can't live like this any more!" Jodie screamed. "I'm sick of being bullied! If I would have slept here last night I would be dead right now!"

"I'm going to call the police," Maddie said. "This is uncalled for!"

"You can't, Maddie. They'll take me away!" She clinched her fist as the muscles in her face tightened. She grabbed her jacket, threw it on, and stormed out the door.

168

"Jodie wait," Tara called after her. She knew the reason she'd grabbed the jacket—the pistol was in the pocket.

"Jodanne, don't you dare do something stupid." Maddie followed Tara and Jodie down the hallway.

"I am not living in fear for the rest of my life. He trashed my home and stole all of my jewelry." She stomped out of the building, stopping at the top of the stairs and spinning around to face Tara and Maddie. "Do you know he took the locket that Nicole gave me for Christmas?" Her voiced cracked. "It was the only thing I had left of her. The only thing!" She hurried down the stairs.

"Jodie, what are you going to do? Come on, let's go back inside," Tara's words were rushed. "I have good news. Tommy thinks he can get custody." She was concentrating so hard on convincing Jodie to go back inside she didn't hear the car—until it was too late.

Suddenly, Maddie screamed, "Jodie, watch out." She threw her arms up and jumped in front of Jodie as if to shield her.

The loud shots sounded like explosives going off. Screams filled the air as people ducked for cover. Tara bowed quickly behind the light pole as the silver car zoomed down the street. She glanced back toward where she'd last seen Maddie and Jodie standing. Maddie was sprawled out in a puddle of blood. Jodie was hovered over her, crying uncontrollably. It had happened so fast, Tara thought she was dreaming.

"Someone call an ambulance," Tara screamed toward the spectators that had gathered around.

A guy pushed his way through the crowd. "The ambulance is on the way." He motioned the people to step back. "Stand back, please." He dropped down next to Jodie. "I'm a nurse. Let me check her vital signs." He picked up her limp wrist and checked her pulse. "She's still alive." He leaned down to inspect further.

Jodie's words gushed out, "It's my fault. This is my fault." She shook the guy's shoulder. "You have to save you. You have to! Do you hear me?"

Tara reached down and pulled Jodie away. "Come on, Jodie, let him tend to her."

Jodie stood, bowed her head, and sobbed into her hands. "It should have been me, you know? She stood in front of me. She's always saving me!"

The ambulance sirens were close.

A police car pulled up, and the ambulance was right behind them.

Tara's heartbeat quickened. "What do we say?"

Jodie glanced toward the policemen coming their way. She whispered in between the sobs, "We don't know anything more than all these other people. Just the car color."

The police first made room for the stretcher and the attendants. Jodie leaned forward and asked the attendant if she could ride in the ambulance. The man asked if she was family and when she replied no, he told her it would be best if she followed them to the hospital. She continued to beg the attendant, and the police had to ask her to step away.

Tara feared that Jodie would rip the pistol out of her pocket if they didn't let her ride with Maddie. But thank God, she didn't.

Tara pulled Jodie close to her while she cried. She'd never seen Jodie so upset before. "Let's go make sure Maddie's place is locked up." She led Jodie up the stairs. "Should we ask the policemen to give us a ride to the hospital?"

"No! They'll be asking too many questions." Her eyes narrowed as she lowered her voice, "Someone's going to pay for this!"

"Jodie, don't talk crazy."

"So help me, Snake's going to wish he'd never met me!"

"Maybe Maddie will be okay."

"Even if she is—I'm still going to get even, and I'm going to finalize it once and for all!" She shoved her hands into her pockets.

Tara had no doubt that Jodie was caressing her weapon, vowing to make Snake pay. She was certain Jodie would carry out her intentions. She'd already confronted him once before, so why would she not do it again.

Tara's head was pounding, and her nerves felt like they'd been through a wringing washing machine. *Why couldn't they*

170

have moved sooner? And what was going to happen to kind-hearted Maddie? A single tear fell down her cheek; she quickly brushed it off with the back of her hand before Jodie noticed. The tables now had been turned, and Tara needed to be the strong one this time.

She glanced up toward the ceiling. *Will it ever end?* Her hopeful, glorious day had turned into a disaster.

***

Jodie walked down the narrow corridor toward the vending machine. It was nearly 7:00 p.m., and there was still no indication from the doctors if Maddie was going to live. They'd already performed surgery to remove the bullet, now it was just a matter of time. At least she was stable. She was still unconscious, which had Jodie worried. She wasn't familiar with medical procedures, but they had told her it was normal. She could only hope they knew what they were talking about.

Tara had already left for the evening, so she could help Tommy pack. Jodie was glad she had come with her today. She hadn't been emotionally able to handle the situation at the time, and Tara coaxed her through it. She'd even told the doctors that Jodie was Maddie's granddaughter and the only sole survivor, which Jodie hadn't even thought of. She'd forgotten how medical information is withheld unless you're a family member.

Jodie glanced passed the vending machines toward the Chapel. She didn't know what attracted her to the room, but it was as though a magnet was pulling her in that direction. She stood outside the door for the longest time. Finally, she stepped inside of the room, not exactly sure what to expect. She'd never been in a church, not even to a wedding. She only knew what the inside looked like from images on TV. It looked similar from what she remembered except a lot smaller. The room was empty and the lights were dim. The pews took up most of the space, and fascinating pictures covered the walls. She walked around the room, viewing each picture. She'd heard of Jesus before and knew most of the pictures were supposed to be of him.

She didn't know if it was the pictures, or the atmosphere, but she suddenly felt warm and comfortable. Almost as if she wasn't alone at all. She thought of Tara and her talks about God, and wondered if she could be right. *What if bad things keep happening to me because I don't pray to God?* She eyed the pews suspiciously. She thought of Maddie's frail, lifeless body and wondered *if it was possible.* She didn't hesitate another second. She hurried over to the pew and kneeled like she'd seen on TV. She bowed her head and spoke silently, '*God, I don't know if you know me because I've never prayed before. I apologize for that. I'm just not certain of things, yet. I understand if you don't have time for me, since I've never made time for you in my life. But I have a problem that could destroy me. See, my mother was shot, and my sister ran off with a pimp, and now the only person that has truly loved me is lying upstairs nearly dead.*' She wiped the tears with her sleeve and continued, '*I don't think I could go on living if Maddie dies. She wouldn't have been outside if she wasn't chasing after me. The shot was meant for me, not her. Please don't let her die. I know I've screwed up my life, but I promise, if you let Maddie live, I will change. I will quit drinking and go back to school, even if it means going to foster care. I promise I will straighten my life up.*' The tears were coming more rapidly, and she had to stop to get a tissue out of her purse. She bowed her head back down. '*I will pray to you every night if you'll just let Maddie live. I'll never doubt you again, I promise. I will even go to church. Please, God, if you can hear me, please let Maddie live. She's all I got. Please help her. She needs you. I need you.*'

Jodie was sobbing into her tissue and didn't hear the minister come up from behind.

"Are you okay, miss?" he asked.

"Oh, I'm sorry." She stood, not sure what to do next.

"I didn't mean to interrupt. I was just wondering if you would like me to pray with you."

"No, I'm fine. I need to be going now. Thanks." She turned and rushed out the door before he could respond. For some reason, she suddenly felt guilty, like a kid who'd just got caught

172

cheating on a test. She hadn't done anything wrong, so she didn't know where the guilt feeling was coming from. The door had been opened, so she'd assumed it was okay to go in.

She was eager to see if the praying had worked. She didn't bother with the slow elevator—she hurried toward the stairs. She ran up them while visualizing Maddie sitting up in bed, waiting to scold Jodie for being out after dark. She jogged down the hall toward the nurse's station. Maddie was still in intensive care, so she couldn't just go busting in whenever she wanted.

"I was wondering if there had been any change in Maddie Stutters condition?" she asked the nurse.

A plump woman in her mid-forties with dark curls framed neatly around her face looked up from her clipboard. "I'm sorry, I just checked on her, and there's still no change. You know she may be unconscious for a while. You really ought to go home and try to get some rest."

"Are you sure she's not awake? Maybe you could check one more time."

"You're welcome to peek in at her, but I assure you she's not conscious, yet."

"Okay, thanks." Jodie hesitated. "I'll just wait in the waiting area for a while, and if there's any change, will you come and get me?"

"Sure, honey." The chunky nurse bent back over her chart.

Jodie entered Maddie's room.

A young male nurse was hooking up a machine to her. "We're just running some more tests."

"That's fine. I won't stay. I'll be back later." She glanced at the once lively Maddie lying helplessly in the white hospital bed. Jodie's heart sank. Seeing her like this was the worse thing she'd ever imagined. "I'll be down the hall if she wakes up."

Jodie decided she hadn't given her praying a chance. She hung out in the waiting room for a couple more hours and then moseyed back to the nurse's station. The same nurse informed her again that there had been no change and encouraged her, once again, to go home, but Jodie insisted on staying. Disappointed, Jodie went back to the waiting area. It was empty;

173

most visitors had retired for the evening. She picked out the most comfortable couch to curl up on. She'd only planned to rest her eyes, but before she knew it, she was sound asleep.

She stirred awake as a variety of voices filled the room. She sat up. There were about half dozen people chatting to each other.

She glanced toward the clock on the wall and was surprised to see it was after eight a.m. She'd slept all night without waking.

She suddenly thought of Maddie and jumped to her feet. She hoped that she'd regained consciousness during the night. If they switched nurses, the new nurse wouldn't have known Jodie was in the waiting area.

Sure enough, a different nurse that Jodie didn't recognize was at the station. She was a young, attractive blond, but she didn't seem as friendly as the nurse she'd had the night before. She acted as though Jodie was interrupting whatever she was doing when Jodie asked if there'd been any change.

"If you want to leave a phone number, we'll call you if there's any change. There's no need for you to stick around here all day. It might be days before she is conscious." The nurse picked up the ringing phone and spoke into the receiver, "Hold, please." She held the phone to her chest while waiting for Jodie to reply.

"I don't have a phone. I will just check back later."

The nurse nodded and continued the conversation on the phone.

Jodie didn't wait for the nurse to hang up. She slipped into Maddie's room without permission. She sat quietly beside her.

After several minutes, she slipped Maddie's hand into her own and whispered, "Come on, Maddie, wake up." She waited for her to respond. "You need to wake up, so I can get you out of this dreadful place and take you home. I'll take care of you, and I'll be the best nurse you ever had."

Silence.

Jodie thought of a recent episode of a soap opera she'd seen, where the guy squeezed the girl's hand, and she responded by

174

squeezing back. At the point, she was willing to try anything. She squeezed and waited but still no response.

"I'll be back later," she whispered and leaned forward to kiss Maddie's cheek.

She hurried out of the room and was half way down the hall before she broke. She glanced toward the ceiling, *why aren't you helping me*, she said silently.

She couldn't take it any more. She had to get away from this depressing place. It felt like the walls were closing in. She stepped outside and lit a much-needed cigarette. She inhaled deeply—she'd forgotten that she even smoked until now. She exhaled the smoke, enjoying the light-headed feeling. She found a nearby bench to sit on. She thought of Maddie and all the good times she'd had with her the last few years. She'd been her mother, her grandmother, and her best friend. Jodie couldn't lose her now! She just couldn't. "Damn you, Snake," she mumbled. Before long, she was sobbing again. She looked toward the sky and silently prayed, *if you're really up there, please, please help Maddie*. After a few seconds, she shrugged. *He's not going to help me!*

She knew what she had to do. She just didn't know when she should do it. Maddie could lie up there for weeks before she came conscious. And then again, she still wasn't out of the clear—she could still die, too. Either way, Jodie had to make Snake pay for what he'd done.

Why wait, she thought. She jumped to her feet. He'd pushed her around for the last time. She could play his game, too. She just had to play smarter, and she was prepared to do just that. She headed in the direction of the bus stop. "You haven't seen anything yet," she said under her breath. She knew her impulsive actions could get her in trouble this time, but she simply didn't care anymore.

Chapter Nineteen

Tara shoved the rest of the towels in a box, leaving out a couple to use until they were completely moved. Today was Tommy's last day to work. He'd have the entire week off to move and get organized. They were hoping to be in the new apartment by Wednesday.

Tommy drank the last of his milk and set the glass in the sink. "Have you called the hospital to check on Maddie?"

Tara glanced toward the clock. It was nearly 10:00 a.m. "I think I'm just going to go over there. I need to see how Jodie's doing anyway."

"You're not going out by yourself! If you're ready now, I can drop you off on the way to work. Take your cell phone too."

"Oh, yeah. I almost forgot I had one." She crossed the room and retrieved the phone out of the charger. Tommy had given it to her last night. He'd also got himself one, so they could keep in touch with each other.

"And I want you to stay with Jodie at all times."

"I will." She grabbed her purse off the table. "I hope Maddie's awake."

"Well, don't get your hopes too high. Her age might play a factor in her recovery time."

Tara followed Tommy out the door and to the car. "I know, but Jodie's gone through so much right now; I don't think she could handle losing Maddie, too. She was a mess yesterday."

"I don't blame her. You two girls have been through a lot these last few weeks. I'll be glad to get you out of this neighborhood and away from the gangs." Tommy pulled away from the curve.

"Do you think Snake will find us?"

"I don't think so. We'll be too far away, and you'll be in a different school. Unfortunately, he'll probably move on to some other innocent girls. Those types of guys will never amount to anything."

"I hope I can convince Jodie to go with us." She glanced out the passenger window. "I don't know if she'll want to leave Maddie."

"I wonder why Maddie stays in the neighborhood," Tommy said. "Even with her low income, I'd still think she could find a better neighborhood." His eyes suddenly widened. "You know there was a lower rental apartment building a block over from our new place. I'm going to check out the rates. And if she does pull through, maybe you girls could convince her to move. We could do the physical part for her."

"No wonder my parents always admired you so much. You're always helping people."

"I believe in karma. One day I might be in the same situation, and someone might have to help me."

Fifteen minutes later, Tara was crawling out of the old Ford Escort. "Thanks, Tommy."

"Remember what I said, I don't want you out by yourself and be home before dark. *And* stay away from the windows. I should be off by nine. I plan to come straight home."

"Don't worry, I'll be careful."

"I mean it, Tara. We're so close to getting away from these thugs. Don't take any chances! Oh and here's some money. Take a taxi if you need to. I don't want you walking anywhere." He shoved a twenty in her hand.

"Thanks. I'll be fine, quit worrying." She slammed the door and hurried into the hospital.

She went directly to the nurse's station. A young, slender nurse was coming out of the room. "Excuse me, could you tell me how Maddie Stutters is doing?"

She looked surprised. "Oh..." She glanced up and down the halls as if she was looking for someone else. "I've been trying to locate her granddaughter. I can't seem to find her. Maddie's awake now. She's been conscious for a couple of hours." The nurse moved to the side of the entrance. "Go on in, but limit your visit because she really needs to rest. She's still very weak."

"Of course. Thank you so much." Tara quietly stepped into the room. Maddie was propped up with pillows, staring up at the TV. "Hi, Maddie. How are you?" She crossed over, kissed her on the cheek, and reached for her hand.

"Well, I'm fine, but I'll be a lot better when I get out of this place." She rolled her eyes and nodded toward the tray of uneaten food. "Have you ever eaten hospital food before?" She snarled her nose. "It's awful."

"You're just used to your own good cooking." Tara grinned. She thought Maddie looked good, considering what she'd been through. The bandages were criss-crossed over her shoulder and around her chest. "I don't think I've ever eaten here before but thanks for the warning." She pulled up a chair next to the bed. "So, what are they saying? Are they going to let you go home?"

"Maybe in a day or two if all my tests come back okay."

"Are you in pain?"

"Not at all. They keep me sedated. They had an IV on me, but they removed it."

"I'm so glad you're going to be okay. We were so worried. Does Jodie know you're awake?"

"The nurse said she'd been here earlier, but since I came to, she hasn't been able to find her. She thought maybe she went to get something to eat."

"I bet she did."

The same nurse came back into the room. "You doing okay, Mrs. Stutters?

"I'm fine. Just a little sleepy."

Tara exchanged smiles with the nurse and realized that was her cue to leave. "Well, I better let you rest. I'll try to find Jodie and come back later."

"You don't have to leave," Maddie protested.

178

The nurse interrupted, "You really need to rest now. You can have more visitors later this afternoon."

"Yeah, you don't want to over do it," Tara said. "I'll be back later."

"Are you sure Jodie is okay?" Maddie asked as the wrinkles across her forehead creased.

"I promise, she's okay. She's just worried about you. Maybe she went home to rest a little. I'll find her for you."

"I don't want her to think this is her fault."

"I'll try to convince her of that." Tara waved as she backed toward the door. "I'll be back later. Try to rest now, Maddie," she called out as she exited the room.

Tara first checked the waiting room to see if Jodie was there, although she was certain she wouldn't be. It was empty except for an elderly man and woman watching a news channel. She rode the elevator down to the bottom floor and checked the cafeteria. Again, no luck. She imagined Jodie ran home to rest, eat, and clean up. She wished she'd checked her apartment before going to the hospital. She had just assumed she'd be here.

She suddenly thought of Carlos and realized he didn't have a clue of anything that had happened since yesterday. She hadn't even thought to call him last night. She stepped outside the hospital and dug out the business card he'd slipped her. She quickly dialed his cell phone, and he answered within two rings. She rattled off all that had happened since yesterday and apologized for not calling last night.

"I'm glad Maddie is going to be okay," Carlos said. "So you have no idea where Jodie is now?"

"I'm thinking she might have gone home to eat and rest a little. She still thinks Maddie is unconscious."

"Damn, I hate it that she is by herself, especially since Snake is patiently waiting to pounce on her. He's not going to stop until he gets her. He doesn't care how many people he hurts in the process. He's such a scumbag."

"I'm really getting nervous." Tara wished Jodie had stayed at the hospital.

"Well, she might get pissed at me, but I don't think she needs to be left alone. I'm going to find her," Carlos said.

"You think you can help convince her to come and live with Tommy and me?"

"I'm going to try. I'm going to go by the apartment now and see if she's there."

"I don't know what to do." Tara recalled Tommy's words not to go out alone, but she didn't have much of a choice. "I'm going to catch a taxi and meet you there. Jodie gave me her extra key last night in case of emergency."

"Great. I'll be there in about twenty minutes," Carlos said. "Can you meet me?"

"Yeah, sure. See you then."

Fifteen minutes later, she was crawling out of the taxi, and a few minutes later, she spotted Carlos jogging down the street.

"Hey, we timed that pretty good," he said, panting. "Whew, I'm out of shape."

"At least you're still standing. I'd be falling over if I'd run all that way." She waited for him to catch his breath and then led the way up the stairs. "I hope she's not sleeping."

"I'm just hoping she didn't mean it when she said she didn't want to see me any more," Carlos said.

"Did she tell you about her sister?" Tara banged on Jodie's door.

"Yeah, she briefly mentioned it. She didn't want to talk about it."

She lowered her voice. "Well, I think that is why she was so upset and took it out on you."

"Yeah, maybe."

After a few minutes and no response, Tara dug the key out of her purse, inserted it, and pushed the door open. "Jodie, it's me. Are you here?" She called out loudly, so she wouldn't be shot from sneaking up on her. "Jodie?" She walked toward the bedroom. The apartment was shambles just as they left it.

Carlos shook his head. "Damn, they did destroy this place! Son-of-a-bitch, those little punks!"

180

A quick glance around Jodie's bedroom confirmed that she wasn't there. Tara double-checked her mom's room and the bathroom, but they were empty as she expected.

She met Carlos back in the front room. "Where could she be?"

Carlos shook his head. "I don't know, but I don't like the looks of the situation."

Tara's stomach rumbled. Suddenly, she wasn't sure if her breakfast was going to stay down. "Oh, God, what if he's got to her?" She dropped down on the couch. "I promised Maddie she was okay." She cradled her head in her hands. "I should have stayed with her all night. I shouldn't have gone home."

"Let's not jump ahead. Maybe we should check out Chester's first."

Tara stood. "Sure. Let me leave her a note in case she comes while we're gone." She hurried to the kitchen and rummaged through the drawers until she found a pen and paper. She scribbled a quick note. "Okay, let's go." She took a final glance around the disastrous area and decided she'd help Jodie clean once they found her. *What if they don't find her?* she thought, as a cold chill crept up her spine.

***

Jodie pulled out the page from the phone directory and studied the listings. There were tons of Williams's in New York, but only one on Camden Street, which was two blocks over from Drexel. She'd spent the last two hours having a taxi drive up and down the streets, circling the vicinity of Snake's territory. She'd pretended she was looking for a fictitious bookstore. The cab driver had argued that there was no bookstore in the area, but since he was being paid, he didn't protest too much. She was trying to familiarize herself with the boundaries of Snake's turf but was also looking for a good spot to hide out while she scouted out the area.

She spotted an old doughnut shop that had been boarded up. A loose board covering the basement window convinced her it

181

would be easy to break into. The shop was about a block away from the gang's boundaries and three blocks away from Camden Street. She'd have perfect view of some of the side streets. She waited until the two guys on the corner ducked into a nearby house and then she had the taxi stop to let her out. The driver tried to tell her it wasn't a good area to be wondering around in, but he quickly dismissed his disapproval as soon as she shoved some bills in his hand.

She was certain that the boys on the corner would be back shortly. They probably were just taking a bathroom break or grabbing something to eat. She waited for the taxi to round the corner and then she quickly removed the board from the window. Part of the window was already missing so it was easy to knock out the rest of the glass with the board. She glanced around to make sure no one had heard the glass break. She quickly lowered herself through the window.

As soon as she hit the floor, she realized she'd have to find something to stand on to see out. She tried to adjust her eyes to the dark room but just coming out of the sun made it difficult. She pulled out her lighter and flicked it on. She ducked from a big spider in a cobweb, inches from her head. After a few minutes, her eyes adjusted to the dark. By the looks of the room, it had been boarded up for some time. Spiderwebs danced in the corners, and thick dust lined the bare shelves. A broken stepladder leaned up against the wall. *How fortunate*, she thought. She spotted a broken broom handle in the corner and grabbed it. She knocked the cobwebs down that were dangling from the ceiling, stepping on the spiders as she did.

Jodie pulled off the black stocking cap, tucked it in the back of her jeans, and shook her hair.

She found a cement block underneath one of the shelves and positioned it underneath the broken leg on the ladder. It was a perfect fit. She climbed up one step on the ladder to make sure everything was visible. She stepped down, satisfied at the spot she'd found. She wondered how long it would take someone to realize the board was missing from the window. She tried to place it back so it wasn't as noticeable, but someone with a keen eye would catch it easily.

She stared out the window awhile, but she quickly grew bored and stepped down. She glanced down at her mother's watch. The only thing of her mom's that she had kept and only because it was something she'd needed. It was 2:00 p.m. She was glad she thought to bring some food and drink. She'd grabbed some snacks from the vending machines earlier. She pulled out a bag of chips and a can of pop from her purse. She sat on the lower step of the ladder and thought about the events that had led her to where she was now. She'd never have believed a life could change so drastically so fast if it wouldn't have happened to her. Every time she thought of Nicole, it pained her heart, and when she thought about Maddie lying helplessly up in that hospital bed, it hurt even worse.

She finished the chips and wiped her hands on her jeans. She climbed back up on the step and stared out. The two boys had returned to their post. They were dressed similar to Snake, black clothes and red headbands. One wore black sweats, while the other had on baggy black shorts and high-top Nikes. They both carried two long club-like sticks, which Jodie assumed were used as weapons. For a brief second her heart sank. She stared at the guys' muscular physiques and their rough looking faces. She must be nuts for coming here. She would surely end up dead. *What was I thinking?* That was her problem—she never thought anything through!

She suddenly squatted as Snake and another guy passed by the window going in the direction toward the boys on the corner.

Her heart beat fiercely as she reached for her pistol. She aimed it in his direction. It was a long shot—she could easily miss. She recalled Maddie's limp body falling to the ground as the bullet hit her shoulder, and all the blood that covered the sidewalk. But the very last thing she remembered was looking up and seeing Snake's vile eyes from under the ski mask as the car zoomed down the street. She had no doubt that it had been him, and as much as she wanted to blow his head off right now, the timing was wrong. If she missed, Snake would kill her, and if

183

she did hit him, the others would kill her. She would have to wait. She lowered the gun and watched as Snake exchanged words with the two guys. He then did some kind of special code shake with each of them and went on down the street.

Jodie was sure he was going toward his own house. She knew it would only be a matter of time, and he would be back out. And she would be ready this time. It didn't matter any longer that she was risking her own life. What mattered was making him pay for what he did to Maddie.

She cleared away a spot on the floor and sat down. She wiped at the tears with the back of her sleeve and wondered if Maddie was still alive. She knew she might not ever see Maddie again, and that saddened her deeply, but she couldn't leave now.

If she didn't see another tomorrow, justice would be served— as long as Snake didn't see one either.

Chapter Twenty

Tara sighed, rubbed her brow with the back of her hand, and plopped down in the chair. "I give up. She's not here." This was their fourth trip to Chester's. They'd rotated back and forth between Jodie's apartment and Chester's, and still there was no sign of her. They'd even called the hospital and asked Maddie if Jodie had been there, which had been a huge mistake. Now they had Maddie worried about her.

Carlos paced in front of the pool table. "Damn, I don't know what to do. I wish I had a vehicle." A few seconds later, he threw his hands up. "Screw the vehicle—I'm going to find Snake!"

Tara jumped to her feet. "No, Carlos." She gripped the back of his shoulder. "Not like this. They will kill you." She glanced toward the clock. "At least wait for Bronze and Matt. They said they would be here by five." She'd found Bronze's cell phone number on one of Jodie's notebooks the last time they'd stopped by her apartment, and Tara called and told him that it was urgent that they meet at Chester's.

"It might be too late," Carlos said.

"Yeah, but *you* won't be much help to us if you're *dead*."

"Okay, okay, I'll wait."

"It's only fifteen more minutes," she added. "Why don't you go get a drink and try to calm down?" Although she feared something bad had happened to Jodie, she needed to stay composed for Carlos's sake.

"It's going to take more than a drink to calm me down." He marched toward the bar.

Ten minutes later, Matt arrived, and Bronze showed up shortly after.

Tara quickly explained the situation and all that had happened yesterday.

"Shit, man!" Bronze ran his hand through his hair. "It sounds like Flipper's in some deep shit!"

"And it wouldn't surprise me any if she didn't go after Snake herself," Matt added. "Once she makes up her mind it's hard to persuade her otherwise."

"Yeah, and she can be a vindictive little shit, too," Bronze added.

Carlos finished the beer in his mug and slammed it on the table. "Will you guys help us find her?"

"You bet we will." Matt stood. "I'll drive."

"I need to make a phone call." Bronze pulled out his cell phone and flipped opened the cover. "I'll meet you guys outside." He disappeared around the corner.

"You think we should go back to the same area as last time?" Matt asked.

"I guess we should try there first," Carlos said.

The thought of driving back to that neighborhood petrified Tara, but she knew they didn't have much of choice. "We'll probably get killed!" She shivered as she followed Carlos and Matt out the door. "But she risked her life to save me, so I owe her."

"Well, I didn't come empty handed." Carlos lifted the leg of his jeans to show he had a small pistol tucked in his sock. "If Snake knows where Jodie is…he's going to tell us!"

They piled into the Focus, leaving the front passenger side vacant for Bronze.

"Maybe Maddie shouldn't have given that pistol to Jodie." Tara hadn't meant to voice her thoughts aloud, but it had slipped out.

186

"It wouldn't have mattered," Matt said. "If Flip had her mind made up to find Snake, she would have done it regardless of the weapon she had."

"Well, she's a lot braver than me," Tara said.

"Right now, that's not a good thing!" Carlos frowned and pulled out a pack of cigarettes from his shirt pocket. "I always knew she was different—I just didn't know how different she was." He lit a cigarette. "Don't get me wrong—I'm attracted to her because she is so unique." He blew smoke out and stared out the window. "But she sure does know how to worry the hell out of a person."

Bronze opened the door, threw a pouch on the floor, and crawled in. "Sorry about that." He pulled a revolver from his pouch and laid it in his lap. "I'm ready now."

Matt pulled away from the curb and headed in the direction of Drexel.

Tara's stomach rumbled again, and for a brief second, she thought of calling Tommy and letting him know what was going on, but she quickly decided against it. He would be furious and probably order her to go back to the apartment. He'd been upset last night when he found out that they hadn't told the police the whole story about Snake. He'd said as soon as he found time he was going to the police station and let them know just what was going on. So Tara could imagine what his reaction would be if she told him that they were searching for Jodie in Snake's territory.

As they neared the vicinity, Tara swallowed dryly and rolled down her window to gaze up and down the streets. She placed her hand over her upset stomach. *Oh my, I'm scared to death,* she thought silently. She was grateful that she wasn't alone. She prayed Jodie was okay. Suddenly another thought crossed her mind, *what if Jodie didn't go looking for Snake, but Snake went looking for her—then they wouldn't even be in the area.*

"Look...up ahead. Is that her?" Bronze leaned forward in his seat.

"It is. I can tell by her posture." Although Jodie's backside was all that could be seen, Tara easily recognized her.

187

Carlos leaned forward and gripped the back of the front seat. "What is she doing?

As the car neared, it was obvious what she was doing. She had a gun aimed toward Snake, and it looked like they were exchanging harsh words. Snake was taking steps toward Jodie, as if he was daring her to shoot him.

"Let me out," Carlos shouted as Matt pulled up to the curb.

They all poured out of the car and cautiously advanced toward Jodie.

"Jodie, what are you doing?" Carlos asked.

"Don't do this, Jodie," Tara said.

"Come on, Flipper, let's go shoot some pool," Bronze added.

Jodie didn't flinch. "Leave me alone, guys. I know what I'm doing." She shook the pistol at Snake. "This bastard shot Maddie, he tried to shoot Tara, and I'm tired of him stalking me!"

"You know, bitch, it doesn't matter if you shoot me or not. Because you won't live through the night," Snake hissed.

Carlos clinched his fists and stepped toward Snake. "You scum...I'll kill you with my bare hands."

Bronze held out his hand to stop him. "No, don't. He's not worth prison." He then spoke to Jodie. "He's not worth it. Let's leave. Don't lower yourself to his level."

Tara took a step toward Jodie. Although Jodie's face was red and whelped from tears, the courage she possessed showed through the hardness of her face. "Hey, Maddie's awake, and she's asking for you."

Jodie glanced briefly at Tara and then back toward Snake.

Tara could have sworn that Jodie's face softened with the mention of Maddie.

"Is she going to be okay?" Jodie asked.

"Yes, the doctor said she could go home in a day or two."

"Really?" She glanced toward Tara again. "You're just not saying that, are you?"

"No, it's true. And that's not all. Tommy has found an apartment for Maddie near us and since Tommy is going to get custody of you, you could stay with Maddie and help her get back on her feet. You could go back to school, too." She paused. "It doesn't have to end like this. Please, Jodie, let's go home." Tara suddenly gasped as her eyes traveled passed Jodie and Snake toward about twenty guys dressed in black and red, coming up the street. Some of them were carrying clubs, while others had sticks or knifes. She took a step backwards toward the car as fear engulfed her. She glanced at her other friends—she had no doubt that this was the end for all of them.

***

Everything was happening so fast, Jodie couldn't think straight. She hadn't even meant to jump out of the window and challenge Snake. Her initial plan was to follow him a ways and then confront him when they were away from the area. But as soon as she saw him—all she could think about was what he had done to Maddie! She got so mad that she reacted without thinking. *Damn it, why do I do these things*, she thought silently.

Her heart raced, and her hands trembled as she kept the gun pointed at Snake. She had waited too long to shoot, and now his gang was approaching from behind She glanced toward her own friends. *Why did they have to find me? And now if they are injured or killed, it will be my fault! If only I'd waited at the hospital for Maddie to wake up*, she thought. She hadn't given her prayers enough time to work, and now she was about to create a tragedy!

Out of the corner of her eye, she spotted Carlos and Bronze's pistols tucked in the back of their jeans. Carlos's hand was on his hip just inches from the gun. And she knew he was prepared to draw it—if needed.

"Jodie, Tara, go get in the car and lock the doors, now," Carlos shouted.

Jodie remained frozen. She glanced toward Carlos and then at Snake, who'd already lowered his arms and was grinning from ear to ear.

"I think it's over for you, bitch." Snake held up his hand for his gang to stop, and then he took a step toward Jodie. "You better shoot me now—that is if you think you can!"

Carlos whipped out his pistol and pointed it toward Snake. "You, bastard, I'll kill you if you touch her."

Snake's boys reacted, and Snake once again held up his hand, so the gang wouldn't advance any further. "It's okay, guys." He did some kind of hand signal to his gang. He nodded toward Jodie and her friends. "These bitches have barked up the wrong street, I believe," he taunted. His gang cheered. "I think you both better lower your weapons." He glared at Jodie and Carlos. "Because if you shoot me, these guys are going to trample you down, and if you don't shoot me, they're still going to trample you down." He smirked and the guys cheered again. "You lose either way."

Bronze spoke up, "We don't want any trouble. We'll just get back in our car and drive away." He held up his hands like he was surrendering. "You got to understand, my friend is upset—her mother has died, her sister's missing, and Maddie was like a grandmother to her. We just want to take her home."

Suddenly, roaring motors could be heard in the distance. They were growing nearer.

Jodie's fear escalated as the thunderous noise grew louder until it was directly behind her. She didn't need to turn around; she had no doubt they were motorcycles, and she feared it was more of Snake's gang, trapping them in.

"And I'm not going home without Flipper," Bronze continued. "You see you're not the only one that has friends. I have a few myself."

Jodie, not understanding Bronze's words, glanced behind her and then did a double take. There were at least forty or more bikers dressed in Harley gear. She was dumbfounded! It was obvious, they were Bronze's friends. She glanced toward Bronze—he signaled to the bikers and then winked at Jodie. The twinkle in Bronze's eyes assured her he wasn't going to let anything happen to her. She glanced toward Carlos—he'd lowered his gun and grinned.

190

Jodie stared at Snake, and for the first time, saw him squirm in his own skin. He seemed shocked by the recent intruders.

Snake glanced behind him as if he was making sure his gang still had his back. And there was a slight quiver in his voice when he spoke, "What do you want from us?"

"I want to blow your friggen head off." Jodie's eyes narrowed as she positioned her feet a couple inches apart and cocked her head sideways. She still wanted him dead.

Bronze approached Jodie and cautiously pushed her arm down to her side so the pistol was aiming toward the ground. "No, you don't, Flip." He spoke to Snake, "I want it all to end right now. I want you to leave Jodie and her friends alone from now on."

Snake snorted. "And what if *I* don't?"

Bronze signaled to his friends and they climbed off their bikes and took off their helmets. "Then my friends are going to make sure you're in no condition to ever bother her again."

Jodie knew this was no match for Snake and his gang. Bronze's friends were big burly guys, twice the size of Snake's gang, and twice as many. Even Bronze's arm was twice the size of Snake's.

Snake glanced toward the men behind Jodie and then back at his own gang as if he was sizing them up and weighing his options.

One of the bigger guys in the gang spoke up. "We can take them! Don't back down from them. No one comes to our territory and tells us what to do."

A few of the others cheered while others remained silent.

Snake didn't seem convinced by his friend's words. "Exactly. That's one reason why we shouldn't have any blood shed here. We have family here." He took a step toward Jodie.

Carlos stepped in front of her. "Don't go any closer."

Snake started to retaliate but quickly decided against it. He stepped sideways so Jodie was in his view. He shook his long, slender finger. "You ever come back here again, the war is back on, Flicker or Flipper, or whatever the hell, they call you!" He spun around and motioned his guys to follow him. At first, a few

191

of them protested, but after a few seconds, they all seemed to agree and silently followed behind him.

Jodie stared after the gang until they were out of view. She dropped her gun and clung to Carlos. She cried into his shirt. "I didn't mean to do it." She pulled away and glanced around at her friends. "I didn't mean to get you guys involved. I'm so sorry." She glanced toward the motorcycle dudes securing their helmets, and shook her head in disbelief. She hugged Bronze. "Wow, I need to let you win a game of pool, don't I?" She grinned. "Thanks so much."

"Hey, that's what friends are for." He waved to his friends. "Thanks guys," he called out.

Matt had already started the car and shouted out the window, "Let's get the hell out of here before they change their mind and go get more of their gang."

"I see it didn't take you long," Bronze said to Tara, who'd already climbed in the back seat.

Tara wiped at her tears. "I just want to get out of here and never come back."

Carlos picked up Jodie's pistol and handed it to her. "You shouldn't need this any longer." He grabbed her hand to lead her to the car.

"Wait." She wrapped her arms around his neck. She glanced toward the others patiently waiting in the car and called out to them, "We'll be right there." She turned back to Carlos. "I am so sorry for the way I've been treating you. It's not because I don't like you but because I do. I'm sorry, I can't explain it."

Carlos lifted her chin and kissed her gently on the lips. "You don't have to explain anything. It's all in the past."

Jodie's eyes widened. "You forgive me? Just like that?"

"Forgive you... for what? It's in the past, remember? And we don't discuss the past—only the future." He passionately kissed her.

She melted under his touch. It was as thought they'd never been apart. She knew that he was being sincere, and suddenly, all her negative thinking turned positive. *Why did she always want to shut out the people that cared about her the most?* She'd been

192

so hurt by Nicole that she had hurt someone that she cared about in return. She had no doubt that she was falling in love with Carlos.

"Come on, lovebirds, we need to boogie," Bronze called out.

The chatter in the car was nonstop all the way back to Chester's. Mostly about how Bronze had secretly called his friends and how surprised they'd all been.

Matt parked the car and they climbed out.

"Sorry, guys, but I can't stick around. I need to go to the hospital and see Maddie," Jodie said.

"Come in for a drink and then I'll drive you there," Matt offered.

"I don't know..."

"Hey, you owe me a game of pool." Bronze winked.

"Okay, one game."

"I'm going wherever you're going." Carlos's kissed her hand. "You're not getting rid of me that easy."

She grinned. "I wasn't planning on it." She stopped outside the entrance. "I do need to talk to Tara for a moment and then I'll be right in."

"Okay, you promise you won't take off?"

His eyes twinkled like she'd never seen before, and Jodie hoped the warm fuzzies in the pit of her stomach never strayed again. "I promise." She kissed him and shoved him playfully through the door.

"What's up?" Tara asked with a concerned look.

"I have something to tell you."

"Okay." She glanced around. "Over there." Tara pointed toward the bench.

Jodie sat on the edge of the bench and rested her hands on her knees. "First, I want to thank you for all you and Tommy have been doing for me lately. I've never had a friend before, and certainly, not one willing to take me into their own family." She sighed. "That's more than my own sister would do." Her eyes watered. "I know that's water under the bridge now. Nicole did what she had to do, and under the circumstances, she didn't have much choice. I forgive her now. But you have done so much for

193

me, and I wanted you to know that although I have a hard time expressing my feelings, I really do appreciate it. I'd be going into foster care if it weren't for you.

"It's okay. I know you would do the same for me."

"Maybe now I would, but in the past I wouldn't have. I haven't been a good person. I've just been concerned about my own problems."

"Don't say that. Look what you did for me the night I came to the neighborhood. You can not tell me you were just thinking of yourself that night when you risked your life to save mine."

"Okay, maybe not that night." She smiled and fumbled with the fastener on her purse while searching for the right words. "Something happened last night."

"Yeah?"

"I thought Maddie was going to die."

"But she didn't. She's alive, and she's going to be fine."

"I know, but I thought she was going to die, so I went to the Chapel in the hospital."

Tara's mouth dropped open. "You did?"

"Yeah, and I prayed." She clasped her hands around Tara's. "I prayed hard. I promised God I would straighten up my life if he would let Maddie live." She pulled her hands away and leaned back against the back of the bench. "And he answered my prayers. Me, Jodanne Josephine James." She shook her head. "He heard me, Tara. He really heard me."

"I knew he would. He's always loved you."

Jodie didn't bother to wipe the tears trickling down her cheeks. "But will he forgive me for going so many years without praying?" She reached for Tara's hand again. "And can you forgive me for doubting you?"

She pulled Jodie to her feet. "Of course God will forgive you. And you don't owe me an apology." She hugged Jodie. "Everything's going to be okay now, you'll see." She gripped her elbow and led her toward the entrance.

Jodie glanced upwards. The sun was going down and hints of red and orange glistened in the sky. A single star danced in the

194

distance. *Thank you, God, for not giving up on me,* she thought silently. "You know what, Tara? Life really sucks!"

Tara's smile suddenly faded.

Jodie continued, "But God is good!" A tingling sensation warmed her insides. She knew there would never be any reason for her to stray away again. And now that God was on her side, she was certain she could handle any situation that life threw at her.

The End

www.ingramcontent.com/pod-product-compliance
Lightning Source LLC
Chambersburg PA
CBHW051510170626
46811CB00002B/732